The Devil

The Devil

KEN BRUEN

Minotaur Books ❈ New York

THE DEVIL. Copyright © 2010 by Ken Bruen. All rights reserved. Printed in the United States of America. For information, address St. Martin's Press, 175 Fifth Avenue, New York, N.Y. 10010.

www.minotaurbooks.com

Library of Congress Cataloging-in-Publication Data

Bruen, Ken.
  The devil / Ken Bruen. — 1st U.S. ed.
    p. cm.
  ISBN 978-0-312-64696-7
  1. Taylor, Jack (Fictitious character)—Fiction. 2. Private investigators—Fiction. 3. Murder—Investigation—Fiction. I. Title.
  PR6052.R785D48 2010
  823'.914—dc22

                                                    2010021266

Originally published in Great Britain by Bantam Press, an imprint of Transworld Publishers

First U.S. Edition: September 2010

10 9 8 7 6 5 4 3 2 1

For Martin Quinn, our best mayor,
and Mark Roberts, our best singer-songwriter.

The Divil – Irish pronunciation of the Devil,
used as a figure of fun,
or with more than a slight sense of trepidation.

Prologue

'Nightmares are the dress rehearsal for the dread awaiting.'

KB

I should be in America.

Tried.

Jaysus wept. Did I ever?

Went to the airport.

Bought my duty-free.

Doing good, right?

Had my one suit on, the black job that had seen too many funerals.

White shirt, muted tie.

I like that . . . *muted*.

Seems almost like a Brit.

Dark one I bought in the charity shop.

I was Xanaxed to the hilt, so mellow I certainly was.

Headed for Homeland Security.

American Immigration.

Seemed to be doing OK, did the eyeballing job, stared into that security camera, then did the index-finger job.

'Now sir, your left hand.'

And you're trying not to sweat like a bastard.

That icy politeness puts me on alert.

Not even 10 mg of Xanax can stop that.

Then the hesitation.

And the dreaded words, 'Could you step to the side, sir?'

You're fucked.

Seems my past was up there, a brief stay in jail when I put a child-beating bollix through a glass window.

I don't regret that, didn't then, don't now.

I was sorry it was on record.

Then I was told I could re-apply for entry to the USA, but for now, sayonara.

The looks from the other passengers, looks of 'Thank fuck it's not me.'

Reclaiming my luggage, returning the duty-free, need I say how that felt?

Shame.

No worse feeling in the whole damn universe.

I finally got back to the general population.

Yeah, just like prison.

I did what you do when you are humiliated.

What I do, anyway.

I went to the bar.

Hadn't been drinking for nigh on six months.

The bar guy would just have to be an asshole.

That kind of day.

Ignored me for ten minutes.

And I seethed.

Watched him polish glasses, wipe down the counter, and finally,

Golly gosh,
He noticed me.
Opened with,
'What would sir's pleasure be?'
His balls for openers.
I went with,
'Double Jameson, no ice, pint of the black.'
I figure something in my tone backed him off and he said,
'Of course.'
I drained the Jay, fast and furious.
Good title for a movie, I thought.
Sat back and waited for the hit.
It came.
The warmth in your belly, the creeping illusion that everything might be OK.
Why you drink the shite, I suppose.
The best bit then.
As it snuggles up in your gut, you take the head off the Guinness.

The bar guy might be a prick but he sure could pour a pint.

Nowadays, we had so many non-nationals in the service industry, they poured a pint of G like a pint of friggin' lager.

This guy knew his stuff, had let it sit for nigh on four minutes before he creamed the head.

I let out my breath.

Hadn't even known I'd been holding it for six months.

You're a dry alcoholic, that's how you live.

And this is wrestling with the Xanax, you're going to get some moments of reprieve.

Take it where you park it.

I hadn't even known a guy had slid on to the stool beside me, till he spoke.

Going,

'Sure is hell here today.'

I was mellow enough now to turn and look at him.

Tall slender man, in a beautiful suit.

You been shopping in charity shops as long as I have, you know the real deal.

This was it.

Armani or some other way-out-of-my-reach number.

The kind of suit, you kick the be-jaysus out of it, it's still there in the morning, like a faded butler, looking prim and proper.

He had long hair, blond with highlights, and, I'd have to admit, a handsome face, but something . . . off.

Maybe the mean, down-turned mouth.

I'd seen enough of them to know they are very bad news.

And obviously he worked out, you could see the toned muscle behind the shining white shirt.

He had a devastating smile, marred a little by two crooked teeth.

And his cologne, top of the range I'm sure, but underneath, something else, like garlic left too long in the sun.

I nodded.

And he asked,

'Travelling today?'

I wanted to say,

'The fuck is it to you?'

but the Xanax, mixing with the booze, said,

'No, change of plans.'

He gave that killer smile again, said,

'Ah, that's a sin.'

His emphasis on *sin* was, I swear, deliberate.

He had the bar guy hopping, no mean feat, ordered a gin and tonic and then, to me,

'Get you something, Jack?'

I said I was good.

Fuck, I was close to lights out but not quite out of it, asked,

'How'd you know my name?'

Ravishing smile and he indicated my dead ticket on the bar, said,

'Says so on your ticket.'

Then he gave a tiny smile, said,

'I met a guy on the plane, you know how it goes, you have a drink or two and get to shoot the shit?'

He paused to see if I was following this.

How difficult was it?

I nodded and he continued,

'This guy was a shrink, and you'll laugh when you hear this, he studied evil.'

I didn't laugh.

He went on,

'So I asked him, you think there is a motive for evil?'

He gauged my response and, seeing nothing special, said,

'The guy tells me evil hones in on those closest to redemption.'

Time for my two cents. I said,

'Lets me off the hook then.'

He gave me the most eerie look, asked,

'You're beyond redemption, Jack?'

Jesus, we were having a drink and he was getting not only theological but downright fucking personal.

I said, letting my bitterness leak all over my words,

'Let me just say, experience has taught me there's no such thing as a free lunch. Or drink, either.'

He made a sound – I blame the booze, the disappointment of non-entry to America, but it seemed like fucking . . . *glee*.

He said,

'I would imagine if evil were zoning in on a person, you'd be the ideal candidate. You have all the requirements for where evil would nest and multiply. Bitterness, disbelief, and a cynical disregard for how such things work.'

I've been around bad guys for a lot of years, some serious whacko jobs, the sociopaths, the psychos, the totally insane. And yet this guy gave me a sense of 'You ain't seen nothing yet!'

But like I said, the blend of stuff in my stomach was keeping me loose. I went with,

'Fascinating as this might appear, I'm not really in the mood for *The Garden of Good and Evil* . . . I never got your name.'

He laughed, a sound like a hyena with meat in its mouth, said, extending his long slender hand,

'I'm Curt.'

I thought he meant his manner – and he was certainly that

– till he added,

'With a K.'

Almost mesmerized by the intensity of his eyes, I echoed,

'Kurt?'

He tossed his long blond tresses, and I mean tossed, said,

'*Absolument.*'

Like I gave a fuck. I was thinking Conrad's *Heart of Darkness*, but being too obvious is never smart so I went with,

'We met before?'

He took a long swig of his gin, savoured it, then said,

'If we had, surely you'd remember?'

I had no reply to this, signalled the barman to hit me again. Kurt said,

'My treat, please.'

I let him . . . treat.

My drinks came and I raised the Jay, said,

'*Slainte.*'

He seemed amused by that, asked,

'That's Irish?'

The tone was as the Brits might say, *sardonic*.

And the feeling he was fucking with me I put down to the booze, so I countered with,

'You're . . . ?'

Meaning,

'Irish you ain't.'

And words failed me.

If I had to guess, he sounded French, sort of, but with a complete mastery of English that was amazing.

He let that hover, that damn smile in place, then,

'I'm of mixed ancestry, far too boring for a man like you to have to bear, but I carry a German passport.'

I decided to stay on the vague interrogatory track, asked,

'You on holiday, business? Leaving or arriving?'

He loved that.

I could literally see his eyes dance with merriment, or as my late mother might have said,

'With devilment.'

He said,

'Business, always working, so many tasks awaiting my attention. I'm currently headed for a city called Galway. Are you familiar with this place?'

He wanted to head fuck, I'd oblige, said,

'No.'

Nothing else.

Almost a Zen response, as my sidekick Stewart would appreciate.

He gave me a long look, impossible to decipher, halfway bemusement, the rest, I think, was anger.

Then he said in that so polished accent,

'A shame, I've rented a rather lovely vehicle and if you'd been going to Galway . . .'

And all of a sudden I was tired of him. Checked my watch, the bus . . . yeah, the bus was about ready to leave. I drained my shot glass, the Guinness following fast.

I stood up and he asked,

'Leaving already?'

I gave him my best look, full of empty promise, said,

'It's been a blast.'

Gave it an American twang to shove it home.

He extended that languid hand again and his grip was fierce. He said,

'I feel we'll meet again.'

Not if I could fucking help it. I left him with,

'Then the jar is on me.'

As I walked away, I could feel his eyes boring into me. Jesus, one creepy guy.

I got outside the terminal and noticed an Aer Lingus lady watching me.

Since our national airline, like the rest of the country, was to hell and gone, it was rare to actually see the green uniform, not to mention an Irish person.

She said,

'I'm sorry to bother you, but are you a friend of the man you were having a drink with?'

The fuck was this?

She read my face, understanding exactly what I was thinking, and continued,

'Since the difficulties with our company, some of us are assigned to just being on site and helping where we can.'

Unless she could get me to America, she was shite out of luck.

I asked,

'Is there a point to this?'

She looked mortified in the way only an Irish woman can, that is, shamed yet defiant.

She said,

'I've been monitoring the departures hall for over a year and I can pretty well read faces now, it passes the time, and earlier I noticed that man due to his striking appearance, and then, I hope this doesn't seem too far fetched, he seemed to zone in on you.'

The bitch was mad, time to get another line of work.

I said, sarcasm all over me words,

'Stalking me?'

She stared at her feet in pure agony for a moment, then the head came up, jaw strong.

'And when you passed through Customs, he actually smiled. As if he knew you'd be . . . re-emerging.'

I gave a bitter laugh, said,

'He was right.'

She was into it now, a whole conspiracy living in front of her, said,

'And he tracked you till you went to the bar, then he's sitting with you.'

I saw the bus approach, tried to keep the irritation to a low, asked,

'Spit it out, what is it you think is going on?'

She ignored my shot, said,

'I'd be very careful of people like that, sir. I grew up in West Cork, the old people believed –'

She was seriously mortified now, but soldiered on,

'– that malevolence is a living, breathing thing and it hovers, waiting for a target, then it latches on, won't let go till it owns you, and usually it targets people who are sad or disappointed. I know this sounds crazy, but that man seemed delighted to see you so . . . despondent.'

Christ, no wonder the national airline had gone down the toilet.

I asked, a mocking tone evident,

'So, the Devil is hanging out in airports, looking for poor bastards who get refused entry to America? And he's what, going to scoop them up? Jesus, lady, you need to get a grip or some serious medication.'

I hurt her badly, wounded her in fact, but for fuck's sake, I was doing her a favour. Wasn't I?

Jesus wept.

I began to move away and she shouted,

'I just thought I should make you aware of the situation. I'm sorry if I sounded odd.'

I gave her a slight smile, nothing too fancy – you can never encourage lunatics – and said,

'Odd? Least you're in the best country for it.'

And oh sweet Jesus, added,

'You need to get out more, take a walk round the car park. You know, get a different perspective.'

I got on the bus, leaving her looking forlorn and lost.

Beyond redemption?

Oddest thing, as the bus swung round to take the turn for Galway, maybe it was a trick of the light, but I thought I saw Kurt pressed up against the glass entry door, not watching me.

Watching her.

1

'May you be in heaven a full half-hour before the Divil knows you're dead.'

Old Irish blessing

Lucifer.

The Light Bringer.

He was the Angel of light.

He believed that man had seriously fucked up.

So, like a good cop, he collected his evidence, brought it to His Lord.

The Lord, being God, like all governments, was highly sceptical and laughed at his bearer of light.

Truly pissed off, like all good cops, Lucifer began to falsify the evidence.

An early fan of *The Wire*, if you will.

Not so much Serpico as Satan.

And yeah, got fucked over.

So he did what you do when you get caught, you rally the guys.

Set up his own shit.

Not quite Mugabe, but he was getting there. His coup failed.

No wonder the Irish have such belief in him.

Failed rebellions.

What we do best.

He was, as they put it, thrown into hell.

And like all former zealots, he swore,

'The fuck I'm going down alone.'

And you kinda have to admire the cojones of the guy. Not only was he taking his motley crew of failed cohorts to hell and beyond, he'd go after God's supposedly mega love.

The Human Race.

He'd enlist:

Idi,

Adolph,

Maggie Thatcher,

And for a pure Trivial Pursuit (even arch demons need recreation) somewhere on the list of crazed cronies he added the name of

Taylor, Jack.

Just for a spot of diversion.

The guy went around with

guilt,

fear,

anger,

spite,

arrogance.

And best of all, he was a half-assed recovering Catholic.

Not only would it give Luc some R and R, he'd get to drink some Jameson, sink a few pints of Guinness and, primarily, watch the stupid bollix try to figure it out.

Where was the downside?

Most diabolical of all, Taylor would look for motivation. That made the Devil laugh out loud. He loved the game most when humans sought explanations and motivation.

Reminded him of wondrous times, like that idiot Aleister Crowley.

And if he knew Taylor, and he sure knew a sitting target, sooner or later, Taylor would do two really stupid acts.

Apart, of course, from trying to understand it.

Taylor would do two incredibly dumb acts.

One: he'd go to a priest.

And by all that is unholy, the priest would feel the wrath of meddling with the Anti-Christ.

And then the tinkers.

Luc had a special hatred for them as the weird clan could *see* things.

He didn't like that.

Not to be seen.

If there was to be a show time, he'd call the time and place.

Mostly, he worried (if such an entity could worry) about them because, unlike Taylor, or priests, or the other minions, they weren't afraid.

He thrived on fear.

His raison d'être, perhaps.

And if Taylor did follow through, with the tinkers, he'd lay such a wrath on them that they'd huddle in the fear he had tried so long to instil in them.

2

'Evil is only a concept to those who've never experienced it. To those who've met it, the term "concept" dropped from their vocabulary.'

KB

Everybody with *an beal bocht* (the poor mouth).

The economy hadn't so much melted as
crashed,
burned
and
died.

Dell had just announced they were pulling out of the country and, of course, a shite load of jobs had gone.

But every single day it was the same dirge, another company was moving operations elsewhere.

The banks were now beginning to understand how the clergy had felt for the past few years, that the next knock on the door was the lynching party.

The government were screaming that in two years we'd be maybe, just maybe, a little bit on the road to recovery.

The beast was no longer slouching towards Bethlehem, he was in full possession and even the wondrous bright flicker of Barack's victory had faded.

I was in Conlon's Fish Restaurant, best fish in the country.

And how they achieved that with us entering the second year of the water being contaminated was a wonder.

The council was proclaiming that it wasn't really the water but the lead pipes, and oddly, 'twas little comfort.

You either boiled all water or bought it bottled.

I was waiting on me

cod

with

mushy peas

and drinking a coffee that tasted like coffee!

I'd almost given up on reading the papers, but Ray Conlon had passed me the *Irish Times*. A photo of a woman killed in a freak accident leaped out at me. A brief paragraph noted how she'd been hit by an unknown car at the car park in Shannon airport.

The photo.

My Aer Lingus woman.

Holy fuck.

I lost me appetite but wouldn't hurt Ray's feelings by bolting.

I wanted a large Jameson.

Fast, wet and lethal.

With the Xanax, I was keeping a sort of lid on me drinking.

A woman was standing over me, asked,

'Jack Taylor?'

Jesus, if I had a Euro for the amount of times this had happened.

And yes, always, always ended in disaster.

My getaway was meant to put all the past horrors of my time as a half-arsed PI behind me.

She was that indeterminate age between forty and fifty, nice face, though looking heavily burdened. Blonde hair pulled tight in a ferocious bun and mild blue eyes that had seen too much of the world.

She fidgeted nervously with her wedding ring, the Claddagh band, and that more than anything else had me say,

'Yes.'

She looked like she was going to fall down, so I offered her the seat opposite.

She took it and I signalled to Ray, who was over in jig time, and I asked,

'May I get you something?'

'Some water would be nice, thank you very much.'

Ray gave me the look and I shrugged.

The fuck did I know?

He brought a bottle of sparkling Galway water, neatly took the top off the bottle and poured half a glass.

She said,

'I hate to bother you, Mr Taylor.'

'Jack.'

She nodded and said,

'I'm Teresa Jordan, a Galwegian too.'

A rare and rarer breed.

I waited.

Spent all my bedraggled life doing that, though for what, I don't know.

She took a delicate sip of the water, then said,

'Noel, my eldest lad, is at NUI – one year left of Science – and he's disappeared. I told the Guards and they said not to worry, *students were always up to shenanigans and he'd show up in his own sweet time.*'

For perhaps the first time in my whole screwed-up relationship with the Guards, I agreed with them.

Easy as I could, I said,

'They are probably right. Students, they get up to mischief.'

I couldn't believe I'd used the word *mischief*.

Evelyn Waugh would love me.

Her eyes fired, and believe me, I've seen it often enough, Irish women do wrath like no other women on the planet.

'He's been missing two weeks, and missed my birthday. Noel would never miss my birthday.'

She did scream that last word.

I took out my notebook, it was for the horses and the latest runners and riders at Lingfield and the Curragh. Adopted my biz tone, like I knew what the fuck I was doing.

'Description, friends, what clothes he might have been wearing, his address, and if possible, a photo.'

A real pro.

Right?

I dutifully took down the data and then she reached in her handbag, took out, like a piece of valued jewellery, a snapshot.

He looked like . . .

A thousand other young kids.

Dark hair, long, lean face with lots of acne, nothing else to say. He was any face you'd see on the street, just an ordinary young student.

She said,

'I don't know what you charge, Mr Taylor, but I have this.'

Handed me a slim envelope. I had the decency or shame not to look inside, said,

'I'll get right on it.'

Took her telephone number and was so relieved when she stood up and said,

'Thank you so much, Mr Taylor.'

I gave her the hollow bullshite about not to worry, I'd get right on it, and finally she was gone.

A new case.

I was working. When the whole country was losing their jobs, I'd just been hired.

Was I delighted?

Was I fuck.

Ray brought my dinner and I'm sure it was up to their usual excellence, but my mind . . . Jesus, that photo, that woman, Shannon airport and my, dare I say, curt response.

I shrugged it off, shouted,

'Ray, got any more tartar sauce?'

This seems too crazy to be true, but within two days of my arrival back in Galway, I'd found a place to live.

A guy I knew was emigrating, like so many, and wanted to rent his apartment.

In Nun's Island!

My previous case had involved nuns and was a bitter and twisted series of events.

I took the apartment.

It overlooked the Salmon Weir Bridge, not that I'd see any of those gorgeous creatures jumping, the poisoned water had killed them off.

It had wood floors, two bedrooms, a tiny kitchen and a large sitting room, crammed with books.

Books.

Always and ever my desperate salvation.

A coffee-maker, washing machine and an internet connection.

What more could you want?

Apart from

love,

care,

purpose,

family,

belonging.

I was so long from any of the above, you think I'd be used to it.

Nope.

Few things as lonely as shopping for one, and eating alone in your own home, aw fuck, that is the pits.

You keep the TV on, the radio in the mornings, just to blank out that awful silence.

As usual, I had me favourite music:

Gretchen Peters,

Johnny Duhan,

Tom Russell.

I had two friends.

Sort of.

Ridge, Ni Iomaire, a gay Guard, who had recently, in a desperate effort for promotion and to *belong*, married an Anglo-Irish landowner, who'd lost his wife and was merely seeking companionship and a mother for his teenage daughter.

How was that working out for her?

How do you think?

Every case I'd worked, she'd been involved and we had a love/hate relationship of the Irish kind. That is, we tore strips off each other, verbally, every chance we got, and yet had saved each other's arses more times than we'd believed possible.

And then there was Stewart.

You want to talk enigmatic?

He'd been a highly successful dope dealer, looked and dressed like an accountant, till his sister was murdered and he engaged me.

By pure fluke, I solved the case. Stewart went to prison on dope charges, back when it seemed like the government gave a shite, and emerged a Zen, deadly, totally unreadable ally.

He and Ridge had paid for my ticket to America.

I'd phoned them and Ridge had said,

'You stupid bollix.'

Stewart went,

'You can travel without moving.'

I preferred Ridge's response.

3

'The Divil loves those who deny his existence.'

Old Irish proverb

I'd barely got started on the case of the student, had asked round and mostly heard he'd been a nose-to-the-grindstone kind of guy.

Sure, he partied at weekends, but seemed to take the idea of getting his degree very seriously.

One girl, a very pretty wee thing, told me,

'Lately, he got involved in ouija boards and all that occult crap, began reading books about Aleister Crowley and shit.'

I was about to say, thank you very much when she added,

'Then he met Lord of the frigging Dance.'

I nearly said,

'Michael Flatley?'

Bit down and waited.

She said,

'Mr K himself, turned up recently and has like . . .'

I'd have sworn she was Irish, but she had that half-arsed American idiom gig going, and sure, used the word *like*.

Like a lot.

I asked,

'And he is? Mr K, I mean, who is he?'

She gave a world-weary sigh that proved she was indeed Irish, then said,

'He preaches some weird bullshite about empowering and the energy of the *the One*.'

I asked,

'Any idea of where I might find the charismatic Mr K?'

She gave a small laugh, no relation to mirth or joy, said,

'That's part of his schtik, he just shows up, begins his tired rap and wallop, a whole bunch of eejits follow.'

I liked her a lot. Women of spirit always appealed to me. I had to know, asked,

'You were never drawn in?'

She gave me the rolling-eye bit, said,

'I work in a fast-food joint to keep me afloat and I hear enough horseshite without having to go looking for it.'

She was Irish, no doubt.

I asked,

'What's he look like?'

She gave it her full concentration, then said,

'Tall, great smile and a shaved head. Hard to place where he's from. He sounds like a German, or maybe French?'

I put out my hand, thanked her profusely and volunteered that she was one bright young lady.

She gave a lovely smile, said,

'My name is Emma, I enjoyed talking with you.'

I spent the best part of a week with students and frequenting student hangouts.

Was even offered some Ecstasy.

The song remained the same.

Noel had been liked, had friends, and then out of the blue – or black – he became a total devotee of this Mr K.

I found no sign of the enigmatic Mr K.

I'd always just missed him.

Or he was due at the Quays and I'd show up.

He didn't.

They found Noel down near the rowing club, hanging by his feet from the flagpole, an inverted cross not so much carved as literally gouged into the skin.

When I called his mother, I left out the above details but had to say it looked like somebody had harmed him.

Fuck, talk about understatement.

Her wails of grief, the sheer torment of her agony made me just want to hang up.

Like I could.

I said the trite shite you do and offered to refund her money.

A silence.

Then,

'Mr Taylor, you use that money to find the scum who robbed me of my precious golden boy.'

I swore I would.

I even sounded like I meant it.

In the local pubs, the murder was on the menu and I heard faint whisperings of the head of a dog being enmeshed in the poor boy's entrails.

I didn't inquire.

Would you?

Fuck, it was sick enough.

While the country went nuts, I went to the cemetery.

Phew-oh.

I sure had a long line of people to pay my respects to.

Cody, my surrogate son, and the others, it grieves me to name them. So many of them in their graves because of my stupidity.

I left my dad till last.

He wasn't buried with my mother.

She'd torn him asunder in life, so at least in eternity, he truly would have some peace.

I did lay a red rose on my mother's grave and tried to think of something nice to say to her.

Nothing.

Not a blessed thing.

Then I walked along the narrow path to my father, and at first, I couldn't register what my eyes were seeing.

Faeces, rubbish, condoms, were scattered over his plot.

Too late to blame my mother.

I was in shock for about five minutes, then began to clear away the debris, and it was then I saw it above my dad's name.

An inverted cross.

You come out of the cemetery and it's but a spit to the nearest pub.

Naturally.

We take our burials almost as seriously as our drinking.

I took a place at the counter and realized I was actually shaking.

The barman, my age, probably used to shook-up mourners, asked quietly,

'What would you like?'

'Jameson, large, pint of Guinness.'

He withdrew discreetly.

Afraid he'd wake the dead?

Once I got on the other side of the drinks, I began to, as the young people say, *chill*.

My anger was at its usual simmering slot and God, I wished I still smoked.

So someone knew I'd been investigating the student's death. Not hard as I'd been all over the campus for a week.

And had sent me a message.

To frighten me off.

By Jaysus.

Made me more determined than ever to find Mr K. Whoever this bollix was, he was a key factor.

There was a blazing log fire in the bar and the temptation to curl up there, get a line of hot toddies going was powerful.

But I turned up the collar of me Garda all-weather coat and headed out.

The barman said,

'God mind how you go.'

My limp was acting up, a legacy of a beating with a hurley.

My heart was going like the hammers and I debated if taking a Xanax would be the wisest course of action.

I took two.

Back in Nun's Island, I thanked Christ that the heating was working and had settled into an armchair when the phone rang.

Ridge.

She made chitchat for a while.

She was even worse at that than me and that's really saying something.

I said,

'What's on your mind?'

She didn't bite my face off, so I guessed she wanted something.

She did.

Her beloved husband was having a soiree on Friday evening, nothing too formal, just sports jacket, tie, slacks!

I was just born for soirees.

I snapped,

'Why?'

She told the truth, I think. Said,

'There are a lot of well-to-do people coming and it would be nice to have an ally.'

I nearly laughed.

We'd been down many roads together, most of them dark, but she'd never used the word 'ally' before.

I could have said,

'You're gay, from a shite poor background and you marry the nearest thing to a fucking lord there is. What did you expect, bliss?'

Instead, I said,

'OK.'

Like I said,

Two Xanax.

I had nearly dozed off when my doorbell rang. I went,

'For fuck's sake.'

Pulled open the door to Stewart. He had some bags in his hands, said,

'I come bearing gifts for your new home.'

Beware of geeks bearing gifts.

He looked wonderful.

The guy I'd once visited in prison was long gone.

At least on the surface.

With his Zen philosophy, designer clothes, laid-back mellow style, he had all the trappings of a hip young entrepreneur.

But he was lethal.

My last case, I'd seen exactly how lethal.

He moved into the living room, said,

'Hey, this is a nice place.'

I said,

'Alas, I'm all out of that decaffeinated tea or herbal shite you drink, so it's either a shot of the Jay or bottled water.'

He volunteered that water would be great.

Jesus, the day a glass of water is that is the day I walk into Loch Corrib.

He settled himself on the couch in the frigging lotus position and I went to get the water. If he was chanting some fucking mantra when I got back, I'd throw him out the window.

He took the glass, then,

'Here are your presents.'
A dressing gown, with the letter J on the pocket,
a dictionary of Zen,
and
green tea capsules.
My fucking cup overfloweth.
I said,
'I'm lost for words.'
I was.
Anyone bearing links to manners, that is.
He was so totally at ease, I wondered how many Xanax
he'd ingested.
He gave me that all-searching gaze I was used to and said,
'So, they wouldn't let you into the States?'
I shrugged as if it didn't matter.
It did.
He asked,
'What now, big guy?'
My chance to surprise. I said,
'I'm on a case.'
He came out of the lotus position, his face truly con-
cerned, said,
'I thought you were all done with that.'
I moved to the window, said,
'I thought I was going to America. Surely Zen covers that
kind of fuck-up?'
He sipped at the water, biding his time, then said,
'Are you going to tell me about it?'
I did.

The whole shebang.

He never interrupted, and when I was done he was shaking his head.

I asked,

'What?'

'Jack, this is real bad karma. Get the hell away from it and finish your investigation.'

I was amused. Just to blow that cool finally I asked,

'What's the big deal? Some shitehead comes after me, I'm looking forward to it.'

He moved from the chair, came and touched my shoulder, said,

'Jack, trust me, this is evil in its truest form. You are not equipped to deal with it.'

I pushed his arm away, turned, said,

'And what about Noel Jordan, and my dad's grave? You think I can let that go?'

His face pleading, he said,

'Jack, I beg you, walk away. You can't do this alone.'

I gave him my best smile, the hundred-watt vibe – pity the teeth aren't my own – said,

'But I've got you.'

Moved to the table, picked up the green tea capsules, added,

'And these.'

4

*'If you are going to sup with the Divil, bring
a long spoon.'*

Old Irish proverb

Come Friday, the gig at Ridge's. She's said to dress casual, mentioning

a sports jacket,

tie.

Like look in my wardrobe, see the black suit, the Garda coat and . . . some jeans and T-shirts.

Time was, I bought all my clobber in charity shops.

I'd have thought with the economic meltdown people would be flocking back to those stores.

Nope.

People were no longer giving stuff to the charity shops!

I headed down to my favourite one, St Vincent de Paul, and the women who worked there had the welcome of the world for me.

I got grey slacks, a snazzy corduroy jacket with leather patches on the sleeves, a Van Heusen shirt and a dark knitted tie.

Cost?

Ten Euro.

I swear to God.

On the bookshelves, I found:

Brian Evanston, with an intro by Peter Straub,

Daniel Woodrell's first two novels

and John Straley's volume of poetry.

Add four Euro to my total bill.

And they thanked me.

I had been really trying to cut down on the booze and even the Xanax, and outside the shop, I got a dizzy spell.

I thought,

'Uh-oh, drop in blood sugar.'

Hoping to fuck that's what it was.

I walked slowly along Merchant's Road. Not many merchants there any more, only the usual luxury apartments. Turned left at the tourist office, which was empty, and into Eyre Square.

Walked up past the Skeffington Arms, which had been renovated and looked quite posh now. Past Abracadabra, who'd given Colin Farrell a free card for life for their fare. After the pub, he'd always fancied a kebab.

I crossed at Holland's newsagents and moved on up to Supermacs.

Galway owner, and fat chips.

What more could you ask?

I went to the counter and reckoned a burger, the big fucker, would bring me levels up, not to mention the fun it would have with my cholesterol.

A pretty girl in the Supermacs T-shirt said,

'How are you?'

OK, I know they're told to be polite, but this?

She added,

'You don't remember me, and me thinking I made such an impression on you.'

The college student I'd talked to, who luckily was wearing a name tag. Emma.

I gave my best laugh, tried,

'Emma, how are you? Didn't recognize you in uniform.'

Did she buy it?

Did she fuck.

Said,

'Yah divil yah, you read my name tag.'

I ordered the burger and she told me to take a seat and she'd be right over.

Worked for me.

It was busy, always is, and I had to share a table with a guy in a bad-fitting suit, munching down on the Philly Steak Sandwich, which was new to the menu, like his life depended on it.

He had the look of somebody who'd got all the bad news there is and recently. Without preamble, as grease dribbled from his mouth, he launched,

'Know why the country is gone to the dogs?'

I had a feeling he was about to tell me.

He did.

Said,

'The fucking non-nationals, you know they get free medical cards? I've worked all me fucking life, do I have a medical card?'

I was guessing no.

But thank Christ, his mobile rang, with one of those awful tunes you can download, like a baby crying.

He muttered,

'Right away.'

Then, grabbing the remains of his Philly, he stood up, said,

'Fuckers won't give you two minutes for lunch, and yeah, a non-national.'

The careless bigotry, now more prevalent, was like a slap in the face.

Emma arrived with the burger and chips, said,

'I added French fries cos you need fattening up.'

I barely stopped meself from correcting her.

French fries?

Chips. Jesus.

But as the Brits say, *that would have been a tad churlish*.

No doubt about it, I was channelling Evelyn Waugh.

I thanked her and then her face fell, literally, as she said,

'Poor Noel, what an awful way to die, the poor creature.'

I could hardly bite down on the burger. I asked,

'What are the students saying, anything to do with Mr K?'

She shook her head, said,

'No one's saying anything, and not a light or a sight of Mr K since.'

She motioned to me to eat my food, saying,

'It will be stone cold.'

I gave it a shot and asked her,

'You're a bright girl, Emma. What do you think?'

She looked at her watch. The place was really jamming up and she stood, said,

'Mind the darkness. Evil rarely appears that on the surface.'

I'd have to hook her up with Stewart.

I'd never seen him with anybody. But then he's never seen me with anybody either.

I liked her, she was that new bright shining face of Ireland, working to pay her way through college, smart, confident and no one's inferior.

My generation, we'd been raised Church-beholden and afraid, and wouldn't have recognized self-esteem if it bit us on the arse.

If we'd had a mantra, it would have been,

'Expect nothing, and by Christ, you're entitled to even less.'

I got outside. The part of the burger I'd eaten had lodged in me stomach like a bad prayer.

I took out my mobile, ruefully thinking,

'If I'd gotten to America, I'd be calling it my cell phone.'

Stewart answered on the second ring.

I asked,

'Are you going to Ridge's . . .' I had to swallow hard and then spit it out. 'Soiree?'

I could hear him laughing and I waited.

He took the hint, said,

'Yes, I'm invited, and would you be needing a lift?'

'If you don't mind.'

I let my resentment pour all over that and he said,

'I'll pick you up at seven, and try to be a bit sober.'

He hung up.

Anthony Bradford-Hemple, now isn't that one hell of a name?

No way you're going to be working in a fast-food joint with a name like that.

Ridge's husband.

I was afraid to join up their names. Hers in Irish, Ni Iomaire.

Jesus, you'd need a prompt card to spit it out.

And worse, I'd been the one who hooked them up.

His daughter, Jennifer, was being threatened and her pony was stolen. I'd got Ridge to check it out, thinking I was helping her away from a dire place she'd reached.

And so, dear reader, she fucking married him.

I could understand her reasoning. As a gay Ban Garda, she was already heavily compromised, and then having a radical mastectomy, she was indeed all out of options.

Sure enough, she got her promotion, was now among the ruling classes.

And mostly, I'd kept my mouth shut.

Comes a horseman, came the dreaded Friday.

I put on my new gear, leaving the jacket till last.

Studied me own self in the mirror, tried to persuade myself that I looked like a slightly befuddled English professor.

Didn't fly.

The doorbell went and there was Stewart, in a fucking Louis Copeland suit. The kind of suit, you roll in the gutter

with it, you come to, that suit is brushing you off, saying,
'You're a player.'
He looked at my gear, said,
'Wow.'
My temper wasn't at its best. I'd only dropped one Xanax
and one shot of Jameson and it wasn't mellowing me out at
all.
I said,
'That is one flash suit, three grand or so, I'd guess.'
He gave his enigmatic smile, said,
'You're close.'
I deliberately moved across the room, glancing briefly at
the nuns' convent – they'd be starting evening rosary –
poured a large Jameson and asked,
'Get you something? I'm fresh out of that decaffeinated
tea, alas.'
He settled himself on the sofa, like a cat, total relaxation,
and I pushed,
'What is it you do again, since you stopped pushing dope,
that affords you the suit?'
He didn't rise to the bait, rarely did, said,
'Jack, I have all sorts of interests and if you ever want to
get your act together, I'd be delighted to have you along.'
I looked at my watch, said,
'We'd better get this over with.'
He got to his feet, his suit without a crease or crinkle, and
added,
'You might have fun.'
As we headed out I said,

'Yeah, and I might get to America someday.'

His car was the new sleek Datsun, grey. Accessorized his suit. He turned the key and pulled effortlessly into the traffic. He hit the tape deck or iPod or whatever and we were blasted by music. I listened in silence for five whole minutes – I know, I counted out the time – and finally asked,

'What on earth is that?'

He turned it up a notch, said,

'Searching for the Wrong-Eyed Jesus.'

There are some lines there is just no reply to.

Ridge's new home was one of those huge sprawling monsters, so beloved by the Anglo-Irish when they ruled the land.

Once impressive, no doubt, but badly in need of repair.

And a bastard to heat.

We drove up a tree-lined path to the main entrance. I asked,

'How many acres you figure he's got?'

Without a beat he said,

'One hundred and fifty-eight.'

'You checked?'

He gave that familiar half-smile, said,

'I check everything.'

Didn't add,

'Reason I have the suit and the car.'

The whole place was lit up, and a bevy of cars were already parked. Stewart reached into the back seat, grabbed flowers and bottles of wine. He looked at me, asked,

'You didn't bring anything?'

I waited till I was out of the car, said,

'Brought you.'

A girl in a maid's uniform welcomed us and offered to take our jackets.

No.

Led us into a large room, with maybe fifty people already lashing into champagne, a huge chandelier overhead and the walls lined with paintings.

We were offered canapés and champagne. I took a glass and Stewart asked for some water.

Ridge emerged from a throng of people, looking radiant.

I've seen her look

like shite,

lost,

angry,

hurt,

but radiant, never.

A blue silk gown made her seem like a beauty.

She hugged Stewart, thanked him for the lovely flowers, then turned to me, said,

'Well, you tried.'

I was a bit taken aback, asked,

'You don't like the jacket?'

She hugged me, a rare and rarer event, and said,

'It's so . . . you.'

The fuck was with that?

There was Anthony Bradford-Hemple and a tall bald-headed man. She told us that her husband was deep

in conversation with a very important prospective client.
Something about him.

The man felt my stare, turned, and I felt a chill. Bald or not, it was the guy from the airport, Kurt.

5

'The Divil knows his own.'

Old Irish proverb

Jesus wept.

I was rooted to the floor.

The blond locks had been shorn, but it was him.

The fuck was going on?

Champagne on top of Xanax and the shots of Jay would screw with anybody's head. Right?

Ridge was pulling at my sleeve, going,

'Jack, are you OK?'

I focused, shook my head and asked her,

'The guy with your, er . . . husband, who is he?'

She threw a fast glance at Stewart. The one that asks,

'Do we need to get him out of here?'

Stewart was no help and she finally said,

'That's Carl Franz. He's arranging for Anthony to turn our home into a tourist resort. He is so amazing.'

Kurt . . . or maybe Carl?

Carl with a K, I'd bet.

Mr K?

Fuck, champagne really does meddle with the brain sockets.

Before I could arrange any of those fevered thoughts into cohesion, they were approaching. I braced meself, resolved to *go with the flow.*

Anthony was all Anglo-Irish cordiality, warmth without conviction, went,

'Jack, so delighted you could make it. May I introduce you to an esteemed prospective business partner, Mr Franz.'

Kurt put out his hand, manners counting most. He said,

'Jack, I've heard so much about you. A wicked pleasure to meet you in the flesh.'

I took his hand, and felt nothing.

Everybody's hand conveys something.

Sweat,

tremors,

warmth,

cold.

His . . . zip, nada, like white space.

And oh my sweet Lord, I remembered the old people saying,

'Shake hands with the Divil, you feel nothing.'

I asked,

'We met before?'

He gave me the eye-fucking look, smiled, said,

'Alas, I don't think so. I'm sure I would remember.'

The tension was palpable and I could see even Anthony looking – what is it the Brits call it? – nonplussed.

But as the story of me bedraggled life, I went with it,

reckoning if they are willing to mind fuck, *bring it on, yah bollix*. I asked,

'You ever heard of a Mr K?'

He gave a tolerant smile to the others, like he could go along with nonsense, said,

'No. Is this a lacking on my part?'

The odd twisted teeth had been fixed, or maybe I was just way off me fucking head.

He let go of my hand and, as luck would have it, the bell sounded for dinner. Ridge grabbed my arm and said, in no uncertain terms,

'Time to eat, Jack.'

And pulled me away.

I didn't look back. I could feel his eyes boring into my head.

Ridge whispered,

'What on earth are you doing? Carl is our bail-out money.'

I shrugged her arm away, said,

'I met the bollix before and trust me, he is the worst news you ever encountered.'

She was livid. Nothing's quite like the fury of an Irishwoman crossed. She hissed,

'Don't you dare make a scene! You taint everything, but you won't do it here.'

I gave her my most honest appraisal, said,

'I'll behave, but mark my words, this guy is the worst news to come down the pike in all our varied history.'

She sighed.

'You'd test the patience of a saint.'

I let that slide.

Dinner was pretty much a blur.

A woman to my left who was shrouded in some perfume that made me gag gave me a full inspection, her eyes telling I was found lacking. She said,

'I'm Mrs Beverley Mahon.'

This was obviously supposed to make you sit up and gasp.

I didn't.

She was, dare I say, a trifle miffed, and persisted,

'Of the Athenry Hunt.'

I fucking love fox hunters.

I drained my glass – some amazing vintage that I'd been told you sip and savour.

Yeah.

I asked,

'Tell me, when you hunt the poor bastard of a fox and the hounds tear it to pieces, do you feel – lemme get the right bon mot – righteous?'

She turned to her other dining companion and I heard her whisper,

'The country is overrun by riff-raff.'

Anthony was table hopping or social networking or whatever they call it.

I needed some air, headed out to the front where the smokers were huddled like the social lepers they'd become. Dark mutterings of a pack of twenty soon costing ten Euro.

The hairs on the back of my neck stood up, not at the

impending rise in cigarette prices but at who I sensed behind me.

'Jack – if I may be so bold as to address you informally – sneaking off for a smoke, are we?'

I turned slowly, needing to get me temper in check, for Ridge's sake if nothing else, and said,

'I quit.'

He was opening a gold cigarette case, drew out, I think you call them cheroots? Silly-looking bastards that are pretending to be cigars. Asked,

'Sure I can't *tempt* you?'

His tone conveying that mocking, jeering lilt.

I said, my voice level,

'Temptation is a young man's gig. I'm way past that shite.'

He lit the cheroot with a gold Zippo, blew a perfect smoke ring, then indicated the dinner progressing behind us.

'Rich food not to your liking, Jack?'

And before I could answer, he said,

'Fast food more your speed, *peut-être?*'

How little I knew then. But full of so much booze, anger, pills, I didn't pay it the attention I should have and went with,

'You're the spitting image of a guy I met recently, except for the hair, or rather lack of.'

He loved that. I could see his eyes dance in delight and he countered,

'The Devil you say.'

And we locked eyes.

Before we could get to the real dance, Ridge appeared. She said,

'There ye are. I'm so glad you two got a chance to have a moment.'

He turned and, I shit you not, took her hand, kissed her fingers, said,

'I think Jack and I will have many moments, but you, my dear, you are ravishing. *C'est vrai.*'

I've had beatings, some very bad ones, and meted out some of me own too, but in me whole bedraggled existence I never wanted to kick the living shite out of anyone as much as that bollix.

Then he offered his arm, said,

'But we mustn't keep your guests deprived of your presence. Shall we?'

I swear by all that's holy, she blushed.

Ridge?

And they were moving.

He shouted back,

'*Mon ami*, till we meet again. *Bonne chance.*'

Good luck?

Good fucking riddance.

I think I had some port and brandy later with Anthony, who told me how delighted he was that Carl and I had got on so . . .

What was the word he used?

I'm afraid to say I think it was *swimmingly.*

And he continued,

'Let me be candid here, Jack.'

When they say that, you know they are going to tell you what a cunt they think you are, but nicely.

'I had thought you to be a bit uncouth, to be honest, I mean no offence here, but a tad common.'

I smiled nicely.

Not a touch common.

And he clapped my shoulder, said,

'But you came up trumps. Carl is very taken with you and I appreciate that, not only on my own account but my dear wife's too.'

Jesus.

For once, I said nothing.

Someone called him and he took his leave, adding,

'I'm someone who doesn't forget his friends, Jack. You bear that in mind.'

I nearly said,

'*Mon ami.*'

We finally got out of there.

I didn't see Carl again, but Ridge gave me a hug and thanked me for behaving me own self.

Stewart and I got in the car, a silence between us till we got some distance from the estate and he accused,

'Why did you tell that guy about my Zen?'

I knew who he meant, but I said,

'What?'

'Carl. He told me I was wasting my energies on the wrong power, that there was a far more powerful force he could introduce me to.'

'I told the fucker nothing about you.'

He looked at me, and for maybe the first time in our varied history he seemed worried. He asked,

'Why is he always using German expressions with me?'

I laughed and then told him about the whole encounter and his continuous use of French with me.

For all his Zen mellowness and outward cool, Stewart didn't like not to be in control. He'd once told me that control was all that saved him in prison.

I told him about the fast-food remark, but we were for once on the same page, in that we laughed it off. I told him of my suspicions about Mr K, the airport guy, and added,

'It sounds like a Dennis Wheatley novel.'

When he asked, Who? I realized yet again I was getting old.

Stewart was back and, I don't know, I felt like we were back in civilization. He said,

'God, I'm glad to be back in town.'

Amen, I thought.

As he dropped me off, he said,

'That guy, he offered to teach me some other paths to power.'

To my endless regret, I said,

'Go for it, string the bollix along, let's see where he's at.'

I was about to shut the car door when Stewart said,

'Jack, I nearly forgot,' reached in the glove compartment, handed me a small parcel, said,

'Because of where you live, I couldn't resist.'

And was gone, burning rubber like the Devil was on his
tail.

I got into the apartment, yet again glad of the heat, and
realized what it was I'd been feeling all that evening.

Cold.

Not just yer average 'I'm friggin' freezing' type hype. But
a deep insidious ice in my psyche.

I put on Sky News.

You live alone, you need sound, by Jaysus, some human
contact, even of the virtual sort.

I popped a Xanax to ease me on down and, what the hell,
poured a small Jameson and then decided to have a hot
toddy.

Boiling water,

brown sugar,

cloves,

hint . . . tiny dollop of the black.

Then of course the Jameson.

God, it was good.

Got me through the horrendous news: lay-offs, despair,
people losing their homes, an unspeakable incest case not
twenty miles from where I was, bank rip-offs, drive-by
shootings in Dublin in front of young children, suicides, and
the impending Oscar ceremonies.

Drink?

Fuck, you'd need to mainline heroin to tolerate the news
these days.

I saw Stewart's package on the table and slowly opened it.

I kid thee not,
ten tiny nuns
and a bowling ball.

I turned off the TV, lined up the tiny nuns and, with an apologetic nod to the convent right outside me window, bowled nuns till I passed out.

Perhaps an ecclesiastical homage to Agatha Christie's *Ten Little Indians*.

Or maybe just God's own noir humour.

6

'The Devil rides out.'

Dennis Wheatley

Did I dream?
   Did I fuck.
   Count the awful ways.
   My dad,
   nuns,
   ten devils lined up to be bowled,
   and,
   get this,
   one dripping ketchup burger.

I woke in drenched sheets, me heart hammering in me chest and that horrendous sense of impending doom.
   I got to the shower, dropping a fast Xanax en route and muttering,
   'Tis the holy all of it.'
   My mouth felt like many cats had shat in there.
   The events of the previous evening were flitting in and out of me mind, like prayers you almost said but forgot the crucial line.

The line that pleaded,

'God help me.'

Shaved without too many cuts and got into a clean white shirt, black 501s, an Aran sweater and moccasins that proclaimed 'Made in Delaware.'

Joe Biden would be delighted.

Turned on the radio to kill the loneliness of an empty home and heard the ex-Taoiseach had been barred from giving a talk at NUI by dissenting students. Bruce Springsteen was publically apologizing for allowing a collection of his hits to be sold at the non-unionized Walmart.

I had to smile at this.

Our own major retail stores were rumoured to have been bought by said Walmart.

Then the death notices.

I usually turned these down as I nearly always knew somebody on the list and it never ceased to depress the living shite out of me.

The local news had an item about a girl, an employee at a fast-food outlet, who had been found dead in a local park.

I stood, shocked to my core.

Couldn't be.

Emma?

No.

What was it the demonic Carl had said to me? Something about fast food?

My heart was pounding and I convinced myself it couldn't be. He wouldn't wage war on me that soon and so up close and personal.

I got the other side of two strong coffees, no milk as I'd forgotten to buy any, and was waiting for the Xanax to weave its magic.

It did.

Calmer, I called Stewart and asked him to check that out.

He said,

'I'm right on it.'

I had a laptop – yeah, me, right up to speed. It belonged to the guy who sublet the apartment to me.

Tried a Google search on the various aliases I'd gotten from Mr K, Carl.

Zip.

Nada.

Not a flogging bite.

Google was down.

Yah believe it?

Due to the appalling weather conditions in London, snow up to their arse, and the freezing conditions had affected Ireland too.

I muttered,

'No biggie, I can live with that.'

Put on me Garda all-weather coat and heavy scarf, gloves, Gore-Tex boots and ventured out.

Jesus, it was cold, and the snow seemed like it might actually stay.

My hangover was hovering, looking for a way in past the Xanax.

I headed for the GBC.

What they call a culchie restaurant. Meaning people up

for the day, from the few farms still in business, frequented it.

Translate as
no pretensions,
no decaff, anything.
Cholesterol heaven.
And it was roasting.
Thank fuck.
The waitress, Cecily, I knew her all me life, said,
'Jack, you look great.'
An outright lie, but you'll take it.
And she asked in that way that only an Irishwoman can,
'Are you perished?'
You live a life like mine, mostly devoid of warmth, you truly recognize it when it greets you.

As long as her type still walked and served the streets of Galway, I'd be able to get out of bed in the morning.

She didn't ask what I'd like. Just brought me
a scalding tea,
hopping toast,
two fried eggs,
two fat sausages,
fried mushrooms,
one crisp rasher,
and black pudding.
Comfort food?
You fecking betcha.
It blows the be-jaysus out of a hangover.
What it does to your arteries, ask the vegans.

I had me mobile with me, primed for what I hoped would not be terrible news from Stewart.

I was halfway into this veritable feast of non-PC food when a woman approached. I thought,

'Oh, for fuck's sake.'

Yeah, she led with the now predictable

'Mr Taylor, I hate to interrupt,' etc.

But the food had done its stuff and I was a little more affable, asked,

'How can I help?' Trying not to think of the previous woman and her dead son.

She sat, nervous, and began,

'This is probably not your area of expertise.'

I would dearly love to know what was, but nodded.

She continued,

'My daughter, she's ten and has Down syndrome.'

I blanked for a moment. Serena May going out that window and all the horror that ensued. But I focused and said,

'Yes?'

'She attends ordinary school and is doing great.'

'That's terrific, good for you and your daughter.'

She bit her lip.

Ah fuck.

I'm a hard arse. I work at it. But that kills me. I asked,

'Her name, your daughter?'

She brightened, went,

'Kelli. She's a wonder, loves school, studies like a nun and is such a contented child.'

Like a nun.

I kept me expression neutral and asked,

'So, what's the problem?'

Now the sadness, in Irish the awful *bronach*.

'A group of girls – all from the same family – torment her, take her lunch money, call her names, tear up her homework and call her a . . .'

She had to pause but I had a horrible idea of what was coming.

'Retard.'

I took a deep breath, my chest congested, fury racing in me blood and said,

'But the teachers, her dad, surely they can do something?'

She began to weep.

Fuck.

And fuck all over again.

Did I need this?

Come on.

I'd been down this ferocious road before and had screwed it up so badly.

She said,

'These girls, their family is very important, nobody wants to be on their wrong side. They can . . . er . . . make trouble for people. My husband, Sean, he's a good man but says he could lose his job, and that Kelli just needs to . . . toughen up.'

I didn't know what to say. Said,

'I don't know what to say.'

She looked into my eyes, pleading, said,

'People say you can do things that others can't.'

Oh sweet Jesus.

She quickly added,

'They live in Salthill.' Then, 'Naturally! Their name is Sawyer and they think they are the bee's knees.'

I wanted to tell her, *Sorry, I can't help you, life is shite, this is how the world goes, yada yada.*

I couldn't.

Lied, said,

'I'll get right on it.'

And she grasped my hand, tears rolling down her face, said,

'Oh Mr Taylor, thank you, thank you.'

And then she was gone.

The fuck was I doing?

Lord knows, and cares less, I'd warrant.

I looked out the window, thinking of Florida and other places I could/should have been. The snow was pelting down and I wanted to stay there, have another cup of scalding tea, finish me rasher, not think of Serena May and Down syndrome.

Cecily approached, asked,

'More tea, Jack?'

I said no, this was fine, and then on impulse asked her – she was an out and out Galwegian and thus a rare species –

'You ever heard of Sawyers in Salthill?'

She gave me an odd look so I pushed,

'What?'

She looked round her, like someone might hear, then leant in, smelling of a really subtle perfume, said,

'Jack, blow-ins – from Dublin, I think, but very dangerous. Stay well away from them.'

And she was gone, with that expression like she'd already said too much.

Tipping is not the practice in Ireland. Like zip codes, we haven't quite got that far. But you know, fuck it, I left twenty Euro, then paid the bill.

As I headed out Cecily shouted,

'God mind you well, Jack.'

Somebody needed to.

7

'My soul was mortgaged so long ago.'

KB

Not sure what exactly to do, I headed for the park where the girl had been found.

The Lord and I don't do a whole lot of biz these days. As Patrick Hamilton wrote, 'Those whom God has deserted are given a bedsit and electric fire in Earl's Court.'

Nun's Island was a long spit from Earl's Court, but the deal was much the same.

Solitary.

I'd tried, even went to Mass for a bit, but it didn't pan out. The collection dish had been passed round and it had an edict on it:

'No coins! Notes only.'

I'd been tempted to write a note to put in there.

And I'd been on my knees in the Claddagh church, begging God to spare the life of my beloved surrogate son.

He didn't.

So I figured I'd muddle through and not bother God a whole lot. He seemed to have important issues, like tsunamis, starvation, etc. to be attending to.

Do I sound bitter?

Like the Americans so nicely put it,

'Fucking A.'

And as if God had indeed heard these ruminations, who should come shambling along but my own clerical nemesis, Father Malachy.

My mother was a bad bitch.

And pious with it.

Gave my dad a dog's life.

That I was, in her words, 'a public disgrace' just added to her martyrdom.

On my dad's death, she leaped into widowhood with glee. The black clothes, the Masses said for him, the whole sanctimonious shite we'd been tolerating for generations.

Some of these widows get dogs or, better yet, a tame priest.

She got the priest. Father Malachy, a chain-smoking nasty bastard who delighted in every fuck-up I had.

And fuck, there were plenty of those.

But you know, the worm turns. He got himself in some serious trouble a while back and came to me for help.

I helped.

Was he grateful?

Was he bollocks.

Seemed to resent me more than ever, proving the old adage, they will never forgive those who help them.

He looked much the same. Nicotine emanating from every pore, his black suit ringed with dandruff, his eyes as unforgiving as any guard in Guantanamo Bay. He stopped, exclaimed,

'I thought we'd seen the back of you.'

I asked,

'You missed me?'

He snorted.

I thought that was some novelistic flourish that literary writers used when they were aiming for the Booker.

But no, that's the sound he made. He said,

'Weren't you all set for America?'

I gave him my best smile.

'I couldn't leave without saying goodbye to you ... *Father*.'

Let sarcasm scald the last word.

He lit an unfiltered cig from the butt of the previous one, inhaled deeply, coughed like his lungs were about to come up, said,

'You broke your sainted mother's heart and you haven't an ounce of repentance in you.'

We'd reached the park, close to the fire station and bordered on the other side by Flaherty's funeral parlour.

All the eventualities covered, you might say.

The Guards had cordoned off the park and that foreboding white tent for a murder scene was in place, with masked and white-suited personnel milling around.

For a moment, Malachy seemed almost human, said,

'The poor girleen, they asked me to administer the Last Rites but tis way too late for that.'

I asked him if he knew who the girl was.

He was still looking at that white tent as if he'd give any-thing not to have to go in there. Still distracted, he said,

'All I know is the poor creature's first name. She was a student, and working in some fast-food place to pay for her books.'

My heart sank. I was afraid to ask.

He added,

'I wish I had a naggin of Paddy. They say her heart was removed.'

I thought for a moment I was going to pass out.

He flicked the cig away, said,

'I better go and do what I can.'

I caught his arm, and if it bothered him he didn't react. I asked,

'Her first name, what was it?'

Without even looking at me, he said,

'Emma.'

And he was moving away.

I grabbed at him, near shouted,

'Who'd do such a thing?'

He didn't even stop, just added,

''Tis the work of the Devil.'

I was rooting in my Garda coat, praying – no, pleading – that I'd brought some pills.

And found the Xanax.

Swallowed one, tried to get my mind in gear.

I began to move away, my emotions in turmoil, a voice in my head screaming, *Oh Jesus no, not that lovely bright girl, the one I've spoken to, had a burger from, please, not her.*

Heard my name called and turned to see an older Guard approaching. Naturally, I figured I was in for a bollocking.

Superintendent Clancy, once my partner, now the top dog in the Force, loathed and despised me. My last case, I'd helped save his young son and I don't think he could forgive himself for being indebted to the person he most detested. His dearest wish was that I drink meself to death, go to America, or both, but get the sweet Jaysus out of his town.

I had tried.

To leave.

The drinking was still under consideration.

Up close, I recognized Sergeant Cullen.

Old school.

I mean by that he lamented the days when you could take a hurley to the thugs who polluted and terrorized the city.

When I had dispensed a certain *justice* in back alleys, he'd actually bought me a drink.

Course, he had to keep his friendship with me a secret and rarely acknowledged me.

We understood each other.

We had once pulled border duty in the days when peace agreements were far in the future, and, under fire in Armagh, we'd been cowering in a ditch, the rain lashing down, and he'd asked me,

'Who the Jaysus is shooting at us?'

A good question in those days.

We'd been armed with batons. Just what you need against Armalites, Kalashnikovs, grenade launchers.

I remember his face even now, a riot of confusion, and he'd added,

'Is it the UVF, our own crowd, or who the fuck is trying to kill us on our own land?'

I said,

'Whoever it is, just thank Christ they can't shoot for shite.'

And he started laughing, hysteria, sure, but he pulled out a flask, said,

'*Uisce beatha.*'

Holy water.

Poteen.

I'd taken a long swig – and that stuff kicks like a nun whose polished floor has been walked on – managed to say,

'Don't worry, this stuff will kill us long before any of the bastards manages to get lucky.'

They kept shooting.

Us? We kept drinking.

To each his own, I guess.

We'd been friends since.

He looked old now, long lines creasing his face, furrows on his forehead you could plant potatoes in.

I'd heard his daughter had been killed by a drunk driver and the accused had walked free, due to emotional problems. I could see that lingering pain in his eyes even now.

I said,

'Sergeant, how are you?'

He glanced back at the scene in the park, said,

'Tis a holy awful business.'

'I hear it's a young student.'

He nodded, still vigilant, lest he be seen talking to me.

That truly saddened me.

Then he composed himself, said,

'Jack, you shouldn't be here. If Clancy knew, well . . .'

I knew.

Then he said,

'I've two years to go to retirement, and to tell you the truth, Jack, I'm just filling in the time. This new violence, the awful savagery, I don't understand it.'

Who did?

I don't know if it's a particular Irish trait or what, but we can only dwell in the darkness for so long without trying to pull something warm out of the inferno. I said,

'Liam Sammon is doing a mighty job with the team.'

And he smiled.

Football, hurling, our last barricades against the tide that is about to engulf us. But it only lasted a brief moment.

He gave me a serious look, asked,

'Jack, you're not involved in any of this? I mean, I heard you gave up all that PI stuff. This is way out of your league.'

Then, almost to himself,

'Way out of ours, too.'

I gave him the old punch on the shoulder we used to use after a fine goal against the likes of Dublin, lied,

'Are yah codding me? I'm getting ready to go to America.'

He stared at my coat, and with a tiny smile said,

'They'll be wanting that back.'

I said with fake levity,

'Good luck with that.'

He adjusted his cap, turned to head back to the carnage, said,

'*A cara, bhi curamach.*' (My friend, be careful.)

I replied,

'A*gus leat fein.*' (You too.)

And more's the Irish pity, neither of us heeded that benign blessing.

A year after that encounter, he was found hanging in his garage, one year short of his retirement.

But a lot of other malevolence was coming down the Galway pike before then.

Somewhere I'd read:

Good which is unused is prone to turn to evil.

I'd gone back to my apartment; the snow had started falling heavily again.

We don't do snow here. It's so rare, we're almost enchanted at the novelty.

Till it starts fucking up transport, heating, our daily lives.

Then we react.

Badly.

And as is our way, we blame somebody.

I turned on the news, almost my penance at this stage.

Banks failing.

The Euro fucked.

And I nearly laughed. In the midst of all this they went local, showing how a new hotel was to be built on the site of the Connacht laundry.

And how wonderful. It would have saunas, hot tubs, tanning booths.

Oh Mother. *Mo croi.*

I went to see how much was left of the Jameson.

I had a real bad feeling it wasn't going to be enough.

8

'Being unwanted is the worst disease.'

Mother Teresa

Next morning, I was all over the frigging place.

Me nerves were shot to ribbons.

I wanted to get right on the Sawyer case, the girls bullying the Down syndrome child. But I knew I was too frazzled to do that with any refinement.

Beating the be-jaysus out of three children wouldn't exactly look good on me next American application.

I had some coffee, real smart I know when yer nerves are dancing jigs along the ceiling.

Did a Xanax, muttered,

'Do some kind of fecking magic, will ye?'

It did.

Took a time, but it got me there.

The snow had eased and there even seemed to be a ray of bright sunshine on the horizon.

As I got me all-weather gear on, I was even able to listen to some music.

Counting Crows.

Johnny Duhan, of course, me beacon always.

And the truly angelic Gretchen Peters.

Song on her album, 'Breakfast At Our House', about the agony of divorce and it was too acute, too accurate, I had to stop it.

The bells for the Angelus tolled.

I stopped, blessed myself.

I was probably one of the last people on the whole damn island who still took the time to say it.

'The Angel of the Lord . . .'

And like the song goes, took some comfort there.

Not from childhood, fuck no. But maybe from that vanished Ireland where people stopped in the streets, blessed themselves and said the prayer.

We'd come a long way.

And gained?

Sweet fuck all.

I tried not to think of that gorgeous girl Emma and her heart torn from her body. The anger and rage literally steamed off me.

I said aloud,

'Get a bloody grip, son.'

Then without another thought, headed out to the pub.

Answers there?

Course not. But at least I could be numb enough not to ask questions.

My mobile rang.

Ridge.

All warmth.

Thanking me for my fine behaviour at the drinks party.

Through gritted teeth, I asked,

'How is Carl?'

Like I gave a fuck.

She gushed. God forgive us both, but she did. Went,

'He is very taken with you. Who'd have guessed you had such charm?'

Who indeed?

She prattled on.

Ridge!

I reined in me animosity, not easy but got there, and she said,

'I hope you don't mind, Jack, but he asked for your mobile number. Was that OK to give it to him? I think he has plans for you.'

I nearly laughed, said,

'You're right, I do believe he has plans for me.'

Then she changed her tune, asked,

'Are you all right, Jack? You sound a bit strained.'

Surely not.

I said,

'Must be a bad connection. But I wonder if I might ask you a wee favour, you being a newly appointed sergeant and all?'

She was still high on the party's success and agreed to do whatever I needed.

Dumb bitch.

I told her about the Sawyers, the little girl Kelli and the bullying.

No problem.

She'd be delighted to straighten them out, and in fact was in town the next day and would appear in full uniform to have a *chat* with the bullying girls. She said,

'Who knows better than you, Jack, the effect of a uniform?'

I felt a pang.

True, me days in uniform, you had a certain presence. Said,

'Thank you so much, I owe you.'

She laughed, said,

''Tis nothing.'

She was so wrong. And ended the call with,

'Jack, I think you've really turned your life around. I'm so proud of you.'

I hung up before she got more ridiculous.

Garavan's, on Shop Street, one of the last remaining old Galway pubs, with an Irish barman.

Wouldn't last.

But I'd appreciate it while it did.

A busker outside was singing 'It's Raining In Baltimore'.

I dropped a ten in his wet tweed cap and he said, in a German accent,

'Zank you.'

The barman thankfully hadn't known of me travel plans, so no need for all the fandango of bullshite. He said,

'Usual?'

I nodded and headed for the snug, a portioned little corner where you can see but not be seen.

The Brits would love it.

The *Irish Independent* was on the table. I scanned the headlines:

1,177 workers lost their jobs every day during January.

327,861 are now out of work.

132,263 posts have been axed since the new Taoiseach came to power.

And the editorial screamed,

'It's going to get worse.'

The barman came over, put down the Jameson first, then the pint of Guinness, nodded at the paper and said,

'I've applied to go to Australia.'

The young people were all heading out again. Like the awful eighties, when our best and our brightest left the dying economy, and never came back.

But tough times bring out the street entrepreneurs.

I'd hardly sank half the Jay before I'd been offered a batch of shirts.

Nearly bought a light blue as it was so like my old Guard's one, but passed when the guy said,

'You can't just buy one.'

The bollix would probably have his own franchise within the year.

I was sinking the black when a woman – Romanian, I'd guess – offered me some DVDs. Said,

'All the blockbusters, sir.'

I flicked through them and smiled.

Hellboy?

Hell, yes.

And

The Reader,
The Wrestler,
London Boulevard,
Abba: the Movie,
Alien vs Predator 2,
Appaloosa.
Said I'd take them all save Abba.
She was surprised, asked,
'You no like Abba?'
Sacrilege?
I asked,
'It's a happy, feel-good one, right?'
She nodded.
And I stared into her gypsy eyes, asked,
'I look to you like a guy who does happy?'
We settled on a price and she was pleased. Then she leant over, said,
'The boy – don't look now, but to your right – he no like you, is true?'
I waited till she'd gone, then casually looked to my right and sure enough, there was a young guy – eighteen, maybe? – sipping a pint bottle of cider, the loony juice, giving me what I can only describe as the Evil Eye.
And his body movements, that jerky motion that spoke of speed jag.
I knew it.
Had, alas, been there.
I checked the sports page.
Robbie Keane, captain of our national team, had

been sold from Liverpool, his big chance blown.

Before I could see why, the jittery kid was sitting opposite me, said,

'Taylor.'

Not a question.

I reached for me pint, not knowing what was on this lunatic's agenda, but at least I'd have something in me hand. I said,

'Help you?' Flexing for the violence that was coming in waves off him.

He smiled. His teeth had been filed down, and he had one of those rings through his nose and really serious sniffles.

Coke rag.

He asked,

'Ever hear of a band named the Devil's Minions?'

I tried to keep it light, said,

'Nope, missed that one.'

He had a battered Tesco bag clutched to his side, and he said,

'Have a look at this.'

Reached into the bag and took out a clear jar of what looked like water. Held it in his right hand. Said,

'You don't know how to mind yer own fucking business, do yah?'

Before I could react, he said,

'But you have an acid tongue, the One says.'

In a moment, he had the top off the jar, said,

'Here's some acid. Don't mess with Our Dark One.'

Threw it in my face.

9

Dia de los muertos.

I clawed at my face in total panic and it took me, I dunno, a lifetime?, to realize it was water.

The shock was almost as bad as if it had been acid.

If.

In my days as a Guard, I'd once seen the result of such an attack on a woman. I was one of the first to arrive and her face was like it had melted. One eye had completely dissolved and bones stuck out at horrendous angles in her screaming face.

What had been her face.

Her mouth was gone and the screams were a high-pitched croon of absolute terror.

A jealous boyfriend.

The courts let him off with a *stern* caution.

My sergeant at the time, true old school, had told me to meet him after work. Said,

'Bring a hurley.'

I did.

He taught me the lesson of the ash.

And that was how I began to appreciate that true justice is dispensed in alleys.

The boyfriend learned sharp and fast, and what I most remember is that neither the sergeant nor I said one single word.

Just used those hurleys till sweat near blinded us.

He took me for a pint after.

Wasn't till we were on the other good side of a few that he finally said,

'You're one hard bastard, Taylor. Where d'you learn to shut yer gob and do the job?'

I told the truth.

'Christian Brothers.'

He laughed, enjoyed that and said,

'Their day is coming. Not even that crowd are above the law.'

Twenty years ago, that seemed unthinkable.

But then, so did *X Factor*.

Now I wiped my face with my sleeve, my whole body threatening to go into shock.

I got out of there. God knows I even brought the DVDs with me.

Headed for the docks.

What used to be the docks before the luxury-apartments bastards ruined them.

Even Padraigeen's, one of the great pubs, was now Sheridan's. With a fucking restaurant.

But no city ever fully goes under.

Drayton's.

You won't find it on the tourist map.
It's not for tourists.
Or
backpackers,
New Agers,
sherry drinkers.
It's for serious business.
Drink,
dope,
and whatever else you're willing to pay the freight on.
It's like the shebeens you used to find up North.
Same feel.
There's not so much a bouncer on the door as a killer
waiting to unleash.
I went to school with him.
He said,
'Jack.'
I nodded.
Inside it was smoky. The no-smoking edict wasn't much
in effect here. There was one simple rule, apart from down-
and-dirty drinking. 'Mind yer own fucking business.'
I got a corner stool at the counter and waited.
Mrs Drayton – yes, there was an actual Drayton – saw
me, and after a few minutes put a pint of the black and a
large Jay before me.
I laid some notes on the counter. Asked,
'How's himself?'
Her husband.
She ignored the money. No one was going to grab it lest

they wanted to lose their arm. She stubbed a hand-rolled on the floor, said,

'Dead, thank Christ.'

I can't say she ever liked anybody. She'd been briefly in the Magdalen laundries, so what did you expect? Oprah?

But she had a kind of odd regard for me. Due mainly to some work I'd done on behalf of the tinkers.

So she lingered.

Then,

'Was there anything else you'd be wanting, Jack?'

I said,

'Some personal protection.'

She never looked around.

You didn't eavesdrop on her conversation, at least not twice. She asked,

'You want people or merchandise?'

'Something easy to carry.'

She gave what might be interpreted as a smile. Headed back to serving some sailors who'd been stranded in Galway for weeks and were waiting payment for two months' service.

If their wages ever came, Mrs Drayton already owned it all.

Maybe thirty minutes later, she placed a Supermacs bag before me. Said,

'Probably smells of chips and vinegar, but I'd say you'd live with that.'

I didn't touch it.

Flashes of Emma, her heart torn out, jagging across my mind.

I heard her say,

'Pay Sean on your way out.'

The bouncer.

I let five minutes lapse then headed for the toilet.

Got a stall and pulled out the bag, a Sig Sauer, full clip.

I shoved it in me jacket then pulled it out, pushed the magazine home and felt, if not better, at least ready.

The price had been written in pencil on the outside of the bag.

Not cheap, but could have been worse.

I wouldn't be paying by credit card.

Back at the counter, I finished my drinks and she approached, held out a bottle cap, said,

'You believe this?'

A bottle cap?

I knew better than to be a smart Alec, waited and she said,

'Turn it over.'

I did.

A gleaming miraculous medal on the inside.

I said,

'*Mhuire an Gras.*' (Mary of Grace).

Handed it back to her, or tried to, and she wrapped her huge work-worn calloused hands round my hand, said,

'You keep it, *gasun.*'

Gasun. Jesus, the Irish for 'boy' but in the most affectionate way.

*

I was on my way back to the apartment and was trying to figure out what all the traffic was doing, all headed for the cathedral. As I was but a prayer from there, it had me puzzled.

Then the bells started ringing and I realized.

The annual Novena.

Nine days of deep devotion, masses at all hours and hordes of people.

It was kind of reassuring that people still believed.

Such a country of contradictions.

Massive unemployment, like we hadn't seen for twenty years.

And the people came to church, donated money like we were still prosperous.

The number-one album in the country was by – I swear to God – the Priests.

No, not some punk band trying for notoriety, but three actual priests, like a celestial Three Tenors.

I got into the apartment just as yet another fall of snow began.

I took my jacket off, put the Sig on the coffee table and looked again at my DVDs. Maybe I'd watch something as I finally grabbed some food.

I sat on the couch, the sudden feel of the acid *manqué* on my face, and shuddered. Mercifully, sleep or exhaustion took me out of the game.

The phone jerked me out of a fitful dream and I lunged for the Sig.

Shook myself and then picked up the phone.

Stewart.

No intro.

'Jack, did you send Ridge on some job?'

Trying to sit up and ease the crick in my neck, I said,

'Er . . . oh yeah, to visit a family in Salthill, to read the riot act to some bullying kids.'

Silence.

I shouted,

'What?'

He sighed, said,

'She's in the hospital, got badly beaten up by some guy.'

Oh holy fuck.

I asked,

'Where is she?'

'In NUI hospital.'

I hung up.

Made some strong coffee, downed two Xanax and splashed water on me bedraggled face. Pulled on my jacket and grabbed the Sig, thinking,

Gotta get some food in sometime.

The bells for the evening Novena were peeling loud.

I muttered,

'Ask not for whom . . .'

It's but a jig and a reel to the hospital from Nun's Island, but the church crowds and the heavy snow made progress slow and by the time I got there, I was sweating like a Cork full back.

I hate hospitals.

Always, always the worst news for me there.

I got to reception and found out that Ridge was on the third floor. Out of intensive care, thank God.

I took the stairs and ran smack into Anthony.

Her husband.

Who grabbed me by my lapels, shouted in my face,

'Taylor, what were you thinking, sending my darling to those thugs?'

His spittle was spattering over my face and I had a flashback of the acid. I brought up both my arms and in one movement not only broke his grip but sent him careening backwards.

I'd had all the shite I could manage for one day.

And worse, as he struggled to keep his balance, I went after him.

Blind rage.

Stewart grabbed me from behind, moved me to one side, whispered,

'Take it easy, Jack.'

Yeah, what I do best.

Easy.

He manoeuvred me into one of those uncomfortable chairs they outbid McDonald's for. Asked,

'Heaven's sake, Jack, what's with you?'

He was kidding?

Nope.

So I near spat,

'He put his fucking hands on me, and I know he's Anglo,

beating peasants is their heirloom, but gee, guess what, we don't take that shite any more.'

Aggression was pouring off me in waves.

Stewart said,

'The seat of your stamina is the *dan tien*, centred just below your navel. Now feel the heat rise to your extremities, and—'

I shut him up.

Fast.

'Keep your *dan* fucking whatever and tell me what happened to Ridge.'

He cast a glance at Anthony, who, I swear to Christ, looked like he was going to come back for more.

I sure hoped he was.

Stewart focused me back, said,

'She went to the home of those children you told her about, in uniform, and was seemingly in mid . . . er . . . admonishment, when the father arrived home. He has, it appears, a somewhat volatile nature and attacked Ridge.'

He had to pause, take a deep breath, then,

'The man was arrested and charged. Normally, you attack a Guard, they throw away the key. You know that, Jack, right?'

There was a *but*.

I already knew what was coming, but waited. He continued,

'Mr Sawyer is already out on bail, his daughters claiming that Ridge slapped them, and you know, the Guards are not exactly in the high esteem they once were, what with that shooting of the boy in Ballyclara, and any suggestion of over-zealous policing is frowned upon. He has the best lawyers, of course, and in fact plays golf with your erstwhile colleague, Chief Clancy, so he will walk, and Ridge may not only lose her stripes, but her job is in jeopardy. You put a young girl on any stand, crying that a Guard slapped her, how's that going to play? So he's laughing at the actual charge, said he may well sue.'

I had a thousand things to reply, all involving heavy profanity, but he added,

'And of course, the fact that she is known to be

a) a friend of yours,

b) gay,

c) suffering post-mastectomy stress . . .

Well, Jack, you do the math.'

I could see her, delighted to be back in uniform, wearing her sergeant's stripes, and God knows, she'd earned them. I said,

'Being in uniform, being a Guard, it has a sense of . . . Jesus, I don't know, purpose. But as a convict, you're probably not that fond of uniforms.'

I wanted to hurt him.

I wanted to hurt somebody.

He was nearest.

He took it. Said,

'We had our own uniform there, the denim. But unlike you, we might have taken it off, but it never quite left us.'

Deep.

Very.

I snapped,

'Fascinating as your prison experiences no doubt are, could we get to Ridge?'

He faltered, only for a second. I'd wounded him. He stood back, said,

'Mr Sawyer broke her nose and some ribs, and kicked her in places where a woman is not really built to be kicked.'

He paused, then,

'Does that bring you up to speed, Garda Taylor?'

His voice was ice.

But did I reel it in, ease up?

Alas.

I asked,

'When can I see her?'

He began to turn away, said,

'Ask the doctor.'

I did finally get to see a doctor, who said she was stable and maybe tomorrow she might be receiving visitors.

I knew I should go and, if not make things right with Stewart, at least make the effort, and Anthony, he was best left alone, I thought. I did give the bottle cap to Stewart, who was horrified. He asked,

'Are you out of your mind completely?'

I said,

'It's for Ridge – turn it over. What is that shite you guys chant? Live in expectation of a miracle. Or as your Zen masters might put it, things are not always what they seem.'

Then I did what I seem to do best, I left.
Nobody shouted,
'Mind how you go.'

10

'The pathetic remnants of a joke called a smile.'

KB

Kelehan's is just across the road from the hospital but is now called the River Inn.

No sign of the river.

It was karaoke night.

Some poor misguided bastard was mangling 'The Impossible Dream'.

I got a double Jay, pint and a corner table.

Hoping to dear God I wouldn't go calling on Mr Sawyer, especially as I had the Sig tucked in me jacket.

I'd tapped into a decent blast of me booze when I felt a man stand over me.

Looked up and by all the serendipity, it was Sergeant Cullen, just about the only friend I had still with the Guards.

But to meet him again so soon?

He asked if he might sit down.

I nodded.

He had a pint of Smithwick's, barely touched, said,

'I'm sorry about Ban Ni Iomaire.'

Ridge – her Irish name. Nearly made me smile.

Nearly.

He said,

'One of the Force gets hit, we gather. But you know that.'

Yeah.

A silence till I said the fucking cliché,

'Bad business.'

And then from nowhere, it all hit me and I felt a panic attack. I excused meself, went to the toilet and threw up in the hand basin, taking the Sig out of my jacket and setting it down on the porcelain. It made a dull metallic thud as it hit.

Looked in the mirror and saw the sergeant behind me. He said,

'Jack, put that away.'

I did.

I washed my face and he handed me a paper towel, said,

'Sawyer is a bad un. Major dope dealer but he has juice, and when he saw Ban Ni Iomaire, he reverted to old ways.'

I sighed, asked,

'And?'

'Well, he's already out on bail, citing police harassment.'

Same old shite.

I asked,

'What, he'll get a wee slap on the wrist and yada fucking yada, right?'

He looked away, couldn't meet my eyes, said,

'He'll run out of luck, but Jack, stay out of this.'

I smiled, said,

'We're missing the best bit of "Impossible Dream".'

*

I went home.

If home is where the heart is, then I simply went back to my latest accommodation.

I kept my mind in neutral, dropped two Xanax, put on one of the DVDs, not even looking at the title.

It was *Doubt*.

Way back when, a young priest, upped on the New Vatican council and all that gung-ho good vibe, was friendly to his students. Till Meryl Streep, as convincing a merciless nun as ever Ireland produced, went after him. Called him a paedophile.

Should have just titled it *Priest*.

Like that would work.

I finally decided it was time I ate and about the one thing I can cook with intent is chilli.

Had all the ingredients and made that baby sing.

Red peppers,

hopping beans,

onions,

garlic,

and what the fuck,

a decent shot of Jay.

If it tasted anything like it was smelling, I was good to go. And it felt good to be doing, if not normal, at least ordinary stuff.

The Xanax kicked and I was chilling, as the young Irish say.

Enough with the heavy shite though.

I ejected *Doubt*, put on *Alien vs Predator* to get some reality into me life.

Found a book of poetry in the closet when I was looking for chives and opened it at random, found these lines:

> . . . that came
> With days
> Being spent
> Too long alone
> A faint yet fainter whisper
> That asked
> To be
> With you
> Those moments
> Before
> The close.

No wonder it was in the closet.

I stopped. I was in the kitchen, but had I heard something come through my letterbox at this hour of the night?

Now we have the best postal guys in the world. But surely not at this time.

I put it down to the mellowness I was experiencing.

On the screen, it sure looked like the predator was kicking the living be-jaysus out of the alien.

I buttered a French roll I didn't even remember buying, but it was vaguely in date, like me life, so what the hell?

Got everything in situ – always wanted to use one of those Latin terms – and moved the feast to the coffee table.

Sat finally, hungry, and out of the corner of my eye, saw an envelope on the mat.

A plain white envelope.

The quandary?

Eat first and sustain the mellow mood,

or

bollix.

I got up, grabbed the envelope, tore it open and a scratch card fell out.

The success and popularity of these items never ceased to astonish me. The latest one I'd heard about, big cash prize, and in times of dire poverty these friggin' things were selling better than ever.

I'd never bought one in me whole life.

Plus a note.

Read:

> Jack,
> Sorry about the over-zealous minion.
> But I have a devilish feeling this scratch is the ONE.
> See you soon.
> Stay away from fast-food joints.
> They clog the arteries.
> K.

I did what you do.

I scratched the card.

The numbers matched.

I'd won 25,000 Euro.

The chilli went cold.

I woke next morning, seriously regretting the chilli.

I was sick as forty dogs and then some.

But the old Xanax.

Sure, it would kick like a frigging mule one of these days. I remembered the pictures of Whitney in the *National Enquirer* a few years back.

I popped two after I threw up what looked like most of the red peppers.

Least I hoped it was them and not some vital organ.

Chilli, unlike revenge, is not a dish best eaten cold.

Pieces of the previous evening started to come back.

In neon.

Jesus.

There's a lot to be said for total blackouts.

As I waited for the X to weave its spell, I got into the shower, turned the bastard to roasting and . . . roasted.

Then tried a very shaky shave.

Let's say it was a wee bit haphazard, but hey, the X was kicking in.

I got dressed:

battered denim shirt to accessorize me battered soul,

a pair of white cords that were one wash away from shredding,

warm sweatshirt that celebrated the Phillies' 2008 win,

me Gore-Tex boots.

The snow hadn't fucked off yet.

Neither had the government.

And then I saw the scratch card.
Had I dreamt that?
Approached it real careful.
Oh my sweet Lord.
Scanned it a dozen times, it didn't change.
I had won twenty-five large, plus the zeros.
I did a little jig, right there on me wooden floor.
Then remembered where it had come from.
The Devil's coin?
Was I literally going to be bought?
By that fuck?
You betcha.
I asked meself,
'What does that make you?'
Maybe the X replied, but I said aloud,
'Fucking loaded is what.'
Hemingway had a handy dictum.
You want to know if something is morally right?
Listen to your stomach.
If it sits like broken glass, then it's morally wrong.
My stomach felt warm and delighted.
I checked the weather – more snow en route – so got me
Garda coat and watch cap.
Headed out.
Claiming me winnings took a bit of time, but I had time,
and waited.
Finally, bingo.
I phoned Stewart.
Not to share the glad tidings of me win.

I was delighted, but not stupid.

He was cold in tone. But what the hell. I tried,

'I was out of line, I'm sorry.'

Silence.

OK.

Then he said,

'Apology accepted, I guess everyone was a little bent out of shape.'

I let that slide.

Touching the Sig in me jacket, I asked,

'How is Ridge?'

Pause.

Then,

'She's doing good, much better than they anticipated. But Jack . . .'

I knew what was coming.

'Might be better if you, er, stayed away.'

I promised I would and then, bloody pushing it, he cautioned,

'And best if you stay away from the Sawyers.'

I bit down, like the Iris DeMent song, and swallowed hard, said,

'Of course.'

He was suspicious, I guess he'd seen me in action too often, said,

'Jack, I worry when you're too agreeable.'

I thought, *Too fucking right mate*. Said,

'Staying away is the best kind of action.'

He took a sharp intake of breath, asked,

'You've been studying Zen?'
I said,
'No, it's from a country song.'
And clicked off.
Sing that, you sanctimonious bollix.

11

'The heart hurts from evil anticipated.'

KB

'So Jack, I don't get this American gig. I mean, come on, what the fuck's with that?'

That line was from Caz, a Romanian in Galway for over ten years.

The Immigration midnight raids, the sudden weekly deportations of non-nationals, he always escaped the net.

Even wangled a job as an interpreter for the Guards and so had all kinds of info.

For a price.

He was as trustworthy as a bent tuppence. We weren't friends, he was too slippery for that and I was too wary. But we had history and a give-and-take dance.

I gave.

And he took, as much as was on the table.

I'd run into him outside the Augustine church, not a breath away from the newest head shop selling Ecstasy due to a loophole in the Irish law.

Seemed kind of apt, both sold mood change, depending on what you believed and especially what you had to spend.

If you managed to skip the church and the head shop, and continued on what used to be a lovely little lane, you hit the sex shop, and not two porno mags from there was, yup, St Vincent de Paul.

There is a wonderful ironic set of inferences in all of that, but I'm fucked if I could be bothered making them.

I was in the church, lighting candles for the recent dead, my old dead and, by the look of things, some yet to come.

I was frustrated by the new automatic candle routine. Vegas without the showgirls. I'm a dinosaur, I know, way past my sell-by date, but is it too much to ask for the old gig of tapers, actually lighting the candle and being connected?

It was my version of comfort food. Candle soup for the soul, if you will.

The whole ritual had a richness to it, a sense of tradition.

And yeah, my candles didn't light.

Like me bedraggled life.

As I came out, I dipped my fingers in the Holy Water font. Surely that wasn't poisoned.

Yet.

Standing on the steps to the church was Caz.

He glanced up at the church, asked,

'Find any grace in there, Jack?'

His accent was more Galway than my own. He had almost classical Romany features, a head of fine black hair, shining in the weak sun, the lively eyes, the chiselled nose, and was dressed in an Aran sweater, last seen on the Clancy Brothers,

the Irish version of the American vest, all tweed and pockets,

and best of all,

the rip-off Barbour wax jacket we were selling to tourists as made in Connemara.

Put him on the Galway hooker – and I do mean the ship we make here, a beautiful craft – and he could be a poster boy for the new Ireland.

Cheap,

fake,

and

smug.

I said,

'Live in expectation of a miracle.'

He liked that.

Gave his best smile, the one that warns, watch your Euros. Two of his teeth were solid gold. In an Irish person, there would be simple gaps. He asked,

'And did you find one, a miracle?'

Hard to dislike him and I'd tried. I said,

'I sure did. Today's the day you get to actually buy me a drink.'

He feigned hurt, but then said,

'Sure, I just got me dole money and the allowance for the three dogs.'

'You have dogs?'

'Don't be an eejit, Jack.'

We paid out for non-nationals to feed imaginary canines

and wouldn't pay our nurses. As Stewart had so delicately put it,

'You do the math.'

No doubt he had the sought-after medical card.

We went to the Front Door, a pub I still have some affection for.

Being contrary, we went in the back.

Don't ask.

I like it, despite the bouncers, those wannabe FBI eejits.

Sign of the times, there was an actual school for bouncers in Salthill.

A weekend course. Guess it only took three days to figure out how to kick the living shite outa some poor bastard and appear justified.

It still managed to vaguely resemble the old pubs and I suppose that's as much as you can expect any more.

We grabbed stools at the counter and a gorgeous girl approached, asked,

'Caz, what can I get you?'

Two pints of Guinness.

She built them slow and easy, a real professional. When she was done, the creamy head on those pints was a work of art. Almost a shame to touch them.

We did.

Caz, toasting '*Slainte amach.*'

He'd garnered enough Irish to wing the important stuff, like toasts, begging and false flattery.

I went with '*Leat fein.*' (And yer own self.)

We put a serious dent in the pints, then he asked,

'How've you been?'

Usually I went with the Galway reply. 'Grand.'

But the truth got in first, said,

'Depressed.'

He signalled the girl and she put two new ones under construction, said,

'Depression is sadness gone riot.'

I was floored. Out of the mouths of babes.

He continued,

'Anyone who can describe depression exactly has never been there.'

Paused, then,

'Because it's beyond words.'

Whatever the fuck was in those pints, he'd nailed it.

His eyes went out of focus and he was somewhere else, said,

'My mother, back in Romania, she was so sad. We didn't know about depression so my father just beat her. She walked into the woods one day and we never saw her again.'

The pints arrived. No money had yet changed hands. I clinked his glass, wanted to say, *Sin an sceal is bronach.* (That is the saddest story.)

But I figured he already knew that.

He snapped back, the artful dodger in play anew. But I went for it, asked,

'Would a demon come after a person – personally?'

You can ask Romanians such things and not feel like a

horse's arse. You ask an Irish person, they'd think you were talking about the Inland Revenue.

He nodded, the cream from the fresh pint on his upper lip, said,

'Oh yeah, first they attach themselves to your family, friends, then through them they claim you.'

I asked the obvious.

'Why?'

'A demon will believe you spoilt some scheme they'd planned and the payback is your soul.'

He gave a bitter laugh, said,

'They seem especially fond of Catholics. The more lapsed the better.'

Jesus Christ, I was afraid to admit the awesome truth of his words. As if sensing my distress, he abruptly changed tack, said,

'Your friend Ridge took a bad beating, I hear.'

I had to remind myself he had the ear of the Guards. He continued,

'The assailant . . .'

Looked at me. I took a long swallow of the excellent pint, waited, then said,

'Was of course charged, and is out on bail.'

I already knew the answer but what the sweet fuck, I asked,

'What will happen?'

He finished his pint in jig time, belched, said,

'Slap on the wrist, claims of provocation and all the good legal argument, and mainly friends in high places.'

Then he asked the question we'd come in on.

'What's this mania for America you have?'

I told him of the time before when Ridge and Stewart got me a ticket, she got sick and I had to defer, then this time was refused entry. But to answer his question I said,

'I loved my dad, he always told me America was the promised land, that you could be who you really were, free of the baggage of the past, and of their deep love of the Irish, their help all through our bedraggled history, and how they took you as you were, not what some gobshite said you were – I thought if I could go there I could be free of all the terrible stuff I've been caught up in, and their books, their attitude, seemed like real freedom to me.'

I was drained.

Hadn't spoken such a full sentence since I took my pledge as a young Guard at the passing-out ceremony at Templemore.

He asked,

'You ever read Anton LaVey?'

I'd never even heard of him and said so.

He smiled, impossible to decipher, said,

'Check him out, he's relevant to our earlier talk. Anyway, he always referred to his homeland as "The United Satanic States of America".'

I was about to mention the demon again when he held up his hand, made the European sign of warding off the Evil Eye, said,

'Jack, don't tell me. I don't want him to take an interest in me.'

As if on cue, his mobile rang. He had that awful ring tone 'I kill you'. Spoke rapidly in what I presume was Romanian, slid off his stool, closed his mobile, said,

'Gotta go, Jack.'

And was gone.

I paid for the pints.

I gave the gorgeous girl a tip and she gave me an icy glare.

Caz leaving abruptly was my fault, she seemed to imply, and I thought she might have a point.

Naturally, I Googled Anton LaVey.

Went 'Oh fuck' as I read.

The night before the first of May is the Satanic festival of Walpurgisnacht. In 1969, an ex-carnival roustabout and part-time crime-scene photographer, LaVey, set up the Church of Satan.

Not a guy for half measures, he plunged right in.

In short order, he got himself a house, painted it black, got a whole new wardrobe in yeah, black, and even purchased a black panther.

The animal, not the movement.

His star seemed to be rising as he gained some brief passing fame with a cameo in *Rosemary's Baby*. And the guy knew how to play the press, leaking them all sorts of lurid stories that led to them dubbing him the Black Pope.

Euphoric on his brief fifteen minutes of infamy, he set up his own church.

Worked for Hubbard.

His gimmick –

Naked altar girls.

An ecclesiastical lap dance before his time.

And it worked.

For a time.

Got Sammy Davis Jr and the then hot-to-trot, Jayne Mansfield.

It blew fast, luridly and tragically.

He had a hard on for Mansfield's lawyer, who knew him for what he was.

And LaVey laid a public curse on the lawyer.

Went badly wrong.

The lawyer died in a car crash, but Mansfield was in the car with him and was horrendously decapitated.

I paused for a moment, lit a cig with the now well-oiled Zippo and couldn't help but think, *Headless canines?*

I stood for a moment, took a Xanax, trying to make some sense of how all this tied in with my situation, then poured a wee Jay, and thus fortified, sat down to read the conclusion.

LaVey died in 1997 in a Catholic hospital. An enterprising reporter named Cathi Unsworth who went on to become a fine novelist discovered LaVey was . . .

Jewish.

12

' "Devil" and "diabolical" come from the Greek word diaballein, *meaning "to slander".'*

I went to a pub in lower Salthill.

Not my usual stomping ground.

It's not quite upmarket.

Yet.

But getting there.

The barman had a dicky bow, but alas, had neglected to iron the almost-white shirt.

I could tell by his eyes, he was probably the best customer.

I ordered a pint. Unlike in the UK, here you don't tip, or ever offer the bar crew a drink. I asked,

'Something for yourself, maybe?'

Large brandy.

I had me guy.

He muttered,

'Normally I don't, you know, but . . .'

I gave him my best smile, said,

'If a man can't have a wee snort now and again.'

He clinked my glass, said,

'*Slainte amach.*'

And threw it back like a man in dire straits.

Straits I knew better than I cared to admit.

I put a fifty note on the counter and his red eyes, the brandy giving them that artificial respite, fell on it eagerly. He put out a hand, said,

'I'm Bob, pleasure to meet you.'

I'd most of me pint gone and he volunteered,

'Another? On the house this time.'

By tea time, he'd be gone.

Once the owner showed up, he'd be so out of the game, it was done but to shoot the poor bastard.

I said,

'Terrific.'

And excused meself to go to the toilet.

Let him wreak havoc on the optics.

Gave him five minutes.

Sitting back on the counter, he was by now my new best mate.

I said,

'You look like a guy who's clued in.'

He rubbed his nose in that way of the doomed coke addict, figuring I wanted to be hooked up, smiled – God, it had been a time since he saw the dentist – said,

'I've been around, could tell some stories.'

I tried to suppress,

'Gotcha.'

Sipped at the fresh pint, let him stew a little, eye the fifty, and then I asked,

'A guy named Sawyer, you know him?'

I won't be daft and say it sobered him, but it definitely got his attention.

He leaned forward, the brandy fumes like a blast of bad news in my face, said,

'Whoa, you don't want to, like, you know, be messing with that dude.'

I waited, touching the fifty lightly with my index finger.

He took a deep breath, then,

'The guy is a major player, got connections, y'know?'

I smiled, us *dudes* just shooting the bull, and asked,

'I was just wondering, as I have a little biz I might put his way and hopefully put a little something your way, in the light of a finder's fee, no one to be the wiser, of course.'

He took the fifty, pushed it in his pocket, said,

'Every day, like clockwork, he plays nine holes, then has a brew or two in the bar, members only.'

Bitterness came off him like rabies as he said that. He knew 'members' was a term he'd never have dealings with.

Half my pint was going sour as the atmosphere went south and I stood, said,

'Be seeing you.'

He was as close to stunned as it gets.

He was at that stage where he was about to lay out his whole shitty life.

He near pleaded,

'You're leaving? I never got your name.'

As I opened the door, I said,

'*Dude*, that's like, cos I didn't give it.'

*

My dad always told me,

'The golf club is not for the likes of us.'

Seeing my crushed face, he'd quickly added,

'But they always need caddies!'

Don't they fucking just?

James Ellroy used to be a caddy.

Need I add more?

But for once, I didn't go blasting in, decided to do this right.

I watched.

For one whole week.

Loitering, you might say.

With serious intent.

Sure enough, my brandy buddy was right. Every day, like jig time, Sawyer played nine holes.

And he cheated.

O.J. Simpson did too and there's a moral there.

Not of any uplift.

Mostly I clocked the two heavies who followed him around.

Big fuckers.

Built to hurt.

He had a drink in the clubhouse after, and then the gorillas drove him home.

One usually sat outside in the BMW. He would have had a Humvee if the market would take it. The second heavy usually stayed at the clubhouse. Minding the clubs, perhaps?

Come three thirty, having safely delivered Sawyer home to

his mansion, the car guy moved off to collect the three daughters, who were no doubt exhausted from a day bullying the wee Down syndrome girleen.

Monitoring a case, following a guy, is just about as tedious as it sounds.

But I stayed with it.

At one point, I even read a discarded cig packet.

The government warning went:

SMOKING MAY REDUCE THE BLOOD FLOW AND
CAUSE IMPOTENCE.

At close to nine Euro a pack of twenty, you'd think nobody would smoke. But the country was still smoking like Bette Davis in her prime.

Broke but fuming.

I kept tabs on Ridge's progress.

She was due to leave the hospital in a day or two.

Figured I wouldn't be on the welcome committee.

Rang Kelli's mother and right off the bat she began,

'Mr Taylor, I'm so sorry your friend got hurt by the father of those girls.'

Her tone.

Something off.

I said,

'She's OK, and as a Guard, she knows to expect trouble in the line of duty.'

She hesitated, then said,

'Well, I so appreciate your time and efforts, and if you send me your bill . . .'

I said,

'The fuck is this?'

Blowing me off?

I could hear her compose herself and then the shite sandwich. She said,

'My husband and I have decided to let the matter go. We may change Kelli's school, but truly, we are so thankful for your time and help.'

I'd take the money, out of pure rage. Gave her my address in very clipped tone, then said,

'Sawyer got to you, didn't he?'

She was nailed. Tried,

'Mr Taylor, really, you've been terrific, but we wish the matter to rest now.'

I asked,

'At the next school, if Kelli has any bullying, what will you do? Let some scumbag scare you off protecting your child?'

She was silent, then said,

'I have to go, but truly, thank you.'

13

'The Devil's mambo.'

Jerry Rodriguez

I got a call from Stewart. He was a little warmer, not a whole lot, but easing up a wee bit. Said,

'I've been trying to get a fix on our Mr Carl, Mr K, or whoever he is.'

I waited and he said,

'He's like some kind of mystery man. I can't find him on any business listing, my usual sources have dried up and not even Google had him.'

I asked,

'What about the students?'

He was rustling paper. A list-maker, was Stewart. I always figured there was something seriously fucking wrong with cunts who made lists.

He said,

nothing,

nada,

zip.

He asked me,

'You hear from him?'

Apart from the money bonanza, not so you'd notice, discounting the acid in me face. I said 'No' and asked about the band, the Devil's Minions.

These he knew. They were a motley crew, no pun intended, and were appearing in the Roisin Dubh the following Wednesday.

Ireland were playing a World Cup qualifier, so the Roisin would be dead.

I said,

'Might wander round there, have a chat with the little bastard who threw the shit in me face.'

He asked if I wanted him to come along and I said,

'Naw, I'm just going to observe. Maybe their Esteemed One will appear.'

He hesitated, knew me too well, then 'fessed up,

'I have a date on Wednesday.'

Just when I'd been reassuring meself he was as solitary as I was, I tried to be happy for him, asked,

'Who's the lucky colleen?'

He didn't want to tell me, I could sense that, then said,

'She's a lawyer . . . er . . . her name is Aine and she . . . well, she likes the things I do.'

Jesus.

Decaff tea,

vegan,

Zen,

clean living.

I said,

'Terrific, have a great time.'

'Thanks, Jack. I think you'd like her.'

Right.

I fucking hated her already.

He rung off, saying he'd continue to dig on our Mr K.

Was I jealous?

Big time.

I was edgy, still watching Sawyer, waiting for the right opportunity. Took two Xanax and headed out.

Bright crisp sunny day.

Go figure.

The snow had just evaporated and people looked, if not happy – too many jobs were being lost for that – definitely relieved that at least the fecking weather had improved.

My mobile rang. I answered and heard,

'Jack – it's OK to use your first name, I hope – it's Carl.'

Dare I say, *Speak of the Devil!*

I said,

'Hi, Carl.'

Breezy.

His accent still foreign tinged, he asked,

'You fancy a bite to eat?'

'Sure.'

'Excellent. The brasserie in Kirwan's Lane does a rather splendid *coq au vin*. Shall we say one o'clock if that suits, *aujourd'hui*? I mean – *excusez-moi* – today?'

I kept with the light banter.

'Works for me, *mon ami*.'

He chuckled nastily, said,

'*Touché*. See you. *A bientôt*.'

I rang off.

Maybe I could nail the fucker down this time.

I checked me watch. Some time to kill so headed for Charly Byrne's.

Jesus, how long since I'd seen Vinny?

Too long.

And there he was, mid banter with some old dear and making her day.

He hadn't cut his hair and still had the look of John Travolta in *Pulp Fiction*. He certainly had the mouth.

When he finally turned he said, I swear by all that's holy,

'Look what the devil dragged in.'

And without further ado added,

'Come in.'

I did.

We had a coffee in Java's. He had his *Irish Times*, his Marlboro Light, putting it out as we entered the café, and for one brief moment, everything was OK.

We got the coffees ordered and a croissant for Vinny, then he sat back, said,

'I thought you'd abandoned us.'

I gave the Irish response:

'Would I ever?'

I told him I was living in Nun's Island and he recommended I read *Sanctuary*.

It was just good to see him.

No flak, no bullshit, just a real long-time friend. I said,

'I'll be needing some books.'

He got out his pen, said,

'Fire away.'

I ordered:

Seamus Smyth, *Quinn* and his new one, *Red Dock*,

Straley,

Gary Phillips,

Jim Nesbitt,

Brian McGilloway,

Adrian McKinty,

Tony Black.

Vinny said,

'Nice list.'

Vinny had much the same upbringing as me save his mum was lovely, but Catholic in all the ways that screwed with you. I asked,

'What do you think of the Devil?'

He laughed – and he is one of the great laughers I know – asked,

'Which Devil had you in mind?'

He was buttering his croissant, laying the butter on with just the right delicacy, and Jesus, it looked tempting. I said,

'No, the real McCoy. Satan, the fire-and-brimstone, cloven hooves and eternal damnation fellah.'

He took a sweet bite of the pastry, relished it, then said,

'I watch *Reaper*, does that count?'

I waited and he added,

'OK, Jack, I can see this is a serious question, so my answer is serious. Look at the state of the country and whoever is stalking the land – it ain't God.'

*

I had time to kill before lunch, so I headed for the main street and heard a guy mutter to his wife,

'Hear about Ryanair?'

She gave him the look of generations of Irish women, sighed, asked,

'What?'

Like she had the slightest interest.

Ryanair, run by Michael O'Leary, was our no-frills, cut-price airline. I admired O'Leary – day after 9/11, he offered free flights to any destination for one cent. I'm not saying he saved the industry, but by Jaysus, he got planes back in the air. I thought he should be running the country.

The man said,

'Ryanair is going to charge to use the toilets.'

The woman gave the universal,

'Hmmmph.'

A sound that men never have and never will understand.

Carl was due to arrive at the restaurant in about half an hour and I had one of me rare bright moments. What the Bible terms *the still, small voice.*

I bought one of those disposable cameras, complete with flash, roll of 24. The radio was on and Keith Finnegan's show was taking a music break. The Killers with 'Human'.

Seemed kind of like an omen.

I went to Kirwan's Lane, passing McDonagh's fish 'n' chip shop, with a line of Americans already waiting. I stationed myself under a canopy that hid me from view.

Saw Carl arrive, strutting along, women turning to watch him.

He knew.

Small smile perched on his handsome face.

He was wearing a light suede jacket that whispered, *serious bucks*, black shirt with a muted red tie, dark slacks and those Loke shoes, handmade jobs I could never afford.

A little sun had emerged and bounced off his bald head like bad karma.

I began to shoot off a whole range of shots, catching him, if not in his full glory, at least in his smug esteem.

He strolled into the brasserie as if he owned it.

For some odd reason, the beautiful words of Francis de Sales' *Cross* crept into my head. I muttered them like some form of incantation.

I knew it by heart. One of the Patrician Brothers had taught me – and I use *taught* with more than a little bitterness.

He beat it into me with the canes they favoured. Those suckers hurt like a bastard.

I can still hear the swish as it came down

again,

again,

again,

palms of my hands, my bare legs, till the sweat rolled down, staining his cassock.

Did I cry?

Not then.

Some might suggest I've been crying ever since.

I used the rest of the roll to shoot the swans in the Claddagh Basin and had a batch of French bread to feed them.

Pocketing the camera and brushing the breadcrumbs off, I headed for the restaurant.

I was thinking about *coq au vin*, and call it a hunch, but I knew it wasn't ever going to be on the menu.

And as it turned out, it wasn't.

During the lunch we had, he never once mentioned it, so did I?

Did I fuck.

I'm not all that sure what it is, except it sounds . . . lewd.

But then I was raised on spuds and cabbage.

Meat was what the priests had.

Later, we discovered, very young meat.

He had the best table.

Quelle surprise.

Rose to greet me. Was he going to embrace me?

Changed to a handshake.

My imagination?

But his hand felt like a dead person's. Waving me to the chair opposite, he said,

'Jack, *bienvenu*. I took the liberty of ordering for us. Champers to start, *n'est-ce pas?*'

Holy fuck.

He clicked his fingers, said,

'*Garçon.*'

The waiter was there in jig time, uncorked the bottle with a flourish, filled our glasses and backed off.

Carl said,

'Moët.'

Is there a reply?

He suddenly produced a fountain pen – Mont Blanc, of course, to accessorize his slim Rolex, no doubt – and held up a finger, motioning me to be quiet.

Jotted down something on a napkin, folded it, put it beside his glass, then said,

'Sorry, Jack, just a business inspiration.'

He raised his glass, toasted,

'Here's to you, fellah.'

Had he now an Irish lilt?

14

'Fear of the inferno drives me to hell.'

KB

Another 'garçon' arrived, with a tray of oysters. Carl said,

'Nothing like a *petit* aphrodisiac.'

I drained my glass, asked,

'You hoping to get laid?'

And before he could respond, I asked the waiter, with exaggerated politeness,

'Could I get a pint of Guinness, *please?*'

Show at least one of us wasn't a wanker.

Carl, not skipping a beat, never looking at the waiter, snapped,

'Make it two and before Tuesday.'

Then grinned at me, said,

'*Mea culpa, mon ami*, oysters without the black would be a sin,' his eyes mocking me.

I was delighted. In the proper mood for down and dirty with this cock-sucker. A level playing field, so to speak.

I waited till the G arrived, then sank half without pre-amble, belched, said,

'Ah, that's the biz.'

He didn't touch his, waved his fingers at the poor bastard hovering, indicating his champagne needed to be refilled.

Time to turkey shoot.

I wiped the froth off my upper lip, said,

'Let's stop fucking around, pal. I know who you are . . .'

Paused.

'And you know I know. So quit the bullshite, what do you want?'

Took a moment, then he threw back his head and laughed out loud, startling the waiters and me.

It was loud. I imagine they could hear him in Purgatory – or Tuam, which amounts to the same thing.

It sounded like a hyena with meat in its mouth.

The hairs on my arms stood up, literally.

Whatever I'd expected –

showdown at noon,

denial,

outrage,

this wasn't it.

He eased down, wiped his eyes, gasped,

'You are, as Mrs Anthony Bradford-Hemple says, priceless.

Did he mean Ridge?

He did.

Continued, the accent changing tone like staccato French, German, whatever the fuck,

'Look at this body of mine, Jack, and you – you broken-down specimen, you poor deluded creature, you seem to

166

believe I'm the Devil incarnate? You are Jack, a one-off, a
true original, no wonder she has a certain fondness for you.'

Ridge, I figured.

An almost grey sheen had entered his eyes, like coal that
would never light unless . . .

He leant back, his body language insinuating languor.

The Devil incarnate seemed to amuse him highly. I was
about to speak but he held up a finger, said,

'Shush. I have, as your esteemed trade unionists say, the
floor.'

He took a delicate sip of the champagne, then said,

'Let's have some fun. Indulge your fanciful delusion for a
moment, act as if *the Devil wears Armani.*'

He leant over, right in my face, whispered,

'I'm the Devil, Lucifer, the Light-Bringer, Lord of
Darkness.'

I said,

'You forgot the apt one, Lord of Lies.'

No smile, he hissed,

'Do not provoke me or allow my superficial courtesy to
mislead you. I've endured a lot of your babble due to your
. . . affliction.'

He waved a beautifully manicured hand at my pint,
continued,

'Be assured of this, my dense disciple. I too have a limited
well of patience, and do tell, *pray* tell, why, if I were the
Devil, why in the name of all that's . . .'

He cackled, completed,

'. . . unholy, would I bother trifling with a wreck such as

you? Surely even a moron like you can appreciate that the Devil must have a busy schedule? Swine flu – so sorry, so non PC, Mexican influenza, recession, Iraq, somewhat pressing engagements, don't you think?'

I said,

'Very eloquent. Here's a thought for you, mate. What if you felt that one jaded, over-the-hill, broken-down wretch had somehow managed to fuck up your malevolent plans? What if, whatever schemes you had for our still Catholic town, what if this wretch somehow managed to keep the one element alive that is contrary to all the Light-Bringer hates?'

He emptied his glass, asked in a tone of pure ice,

'What element might that be, Taylor?'

Taylor? No more Jack?

I smiled, drew out the word, said,

'Hope.'

He stared at me for a long moment then switched gear, muttered something in German, I think, but I'm guessing, said,

'Wasn't that fun? Let me ask you a question, Mr Purveyor of Hope. Have you ever read the Catechism of the Catholic Church, second edition?'

He smiled, added,

'Not to be confused with the Second Coming.'

I said,

'Missed that one. Is it on DVD?'

He was done with me for now, said,

'And you such a vociferous reader? I highly recommend it.'

He paused, licked his lips, said,

'Specifically, look at Section Two! But enough of all this gravitas. If I'm the Devil and you're mankind's hope, the world is even more fucked than one could have dreamed.'

His use of the curse seemed to shake the table.

It certainly shook me.

Much later, I did track down the piece on the internet, titled *The Fall of the Angels*. Dealing with the real enemy of Catholicism, it read:

Behind the disobedient choice of our first parents lurks a seductive voice, opposed to God, which makes them fall into death out of envy. Scripture and the Church's tradition see in this the fallen angel called Satan or Lucifer.

All of a sudden I knew I was outgunned, out of my league, and I just gave up. I'd thought I could play, beat this sucker hands down and not even have to exert meself.

The waiter brought entrées.

Prawn cocktails.

After oysters?

He dug into his with gusto, snapping his fingers for more bubbly. He seemed to have a thirst brought on by the fires of hell.

I stayed with the G.

The Devil you know, right?

I wasn't going to beat him verbally, he had too much sleight of hand for my slower repartee.

The main course arrived.

Steaks.

So rare, the blood was leaking over the edge of the plate. I said to the waiter,

'Sorry, but I need it well done, please.'

Carl smiled, went,

'I'd have pegged you as the raw-meat type.'

I let it simmer, then said,

'You'd have been wrong, *mon ami*.'

He didn't so much eat the steak as devour it. Like some jackal who realizes another predator might show.

When mine arrived, cooked to a crisp, I barely touched it.

Pushing his plate aside, pieces of meat lodged in his teeth, he asked,

'Dessert?'

'No, thanks.'

He signalled for the bill and I made to reach for my wallet but he was already laying a platinum card on the table.

I don't do cards.

And I do know when I've had me arse well and truly kicked.

As the Americans say, *He handed me my ass.*

He knew.

I knew.

So I did what you do when you've been walloped, especially with champagne as an outrider to your defeat.

I shut the fuck up.

We stood to leave and he put his arm round me.

I shit thee not.

I loved that.

There was a time, when I had some mettle, I'd have taken that arm and broken it over me knee and not a moment's sleep would it have cost me.

Now, I adjusted me hearing aid.

Felt my limp kick in.

Made a note to meself, *Give up, root out your K. C. Constantine novels and become a hermit.*

Carl, figuring I was done but to bury me, said,

'I'm going to help you, Jackie.'

Next he'd be calling me Jackie-o.

I asked, quietly,

'How's that?'

He beamed, the cat with all the freaking cream, said,

'I have some, shall we say, juice?'

OJ?

Continued,

'I'm aware of your fervent lust to get to the USA.'

Yeah, he leaned on the L word.

Humble as Bono, I near whispered,

'Really?'

We were on Quay Street now, him literally leading me. He said in a Brit accent,

'Name your departure date, matey.'

I said,

'ASAP.'

He let me go, threw out his arms, bellowed,

'What are you waiting for? Get packing.'

I would.

Next time, I'd be packing the Sig.

We were at the crossroads where Quay Street leads off to three different streets. Carl paused, said,

'Ah, a crossroads. No doubt you're familiar with the story of the blues musician who sold his soul at such a junction?'

I asked,

'Why would I want to sell my soul?'

He slapped my shoulder hard, laughed, said,

'You already have.'

He turned at Naughton's pub, near Judy Green's pottery shop, said,

'*Quel dommage*, but I must bid you adieu.'

A Japanese photo-cluster-fuck was taking snaps of everything and he suddenly bared his teeth, bile in his eyes, said,

'Jack, I hate photographs.'

I stood there, watching him strut off, the Stones song 'Sympathy For The Devil' uncoiling in my head.

I'm paraphrasing here, but it goes something like:

> happy to meet you,
> did you guess me name?

I know those aren't the lyrics, but you get the drift.
I had the film developed at a one-hour photo joint.
The swans came out lovely.
The Claddagh church appeared splendid.
Of Carl, I'd taken, I think, thirteen shots.
All blank.

15

'If the Devil is at my left hand, then who is at my right?'

KB

I got back to me apartment.

Down,

depressed,

defeated.

Nietzsche wrote that 'to shame a man is to kill him'.

No argument from me there.

I opened the door, it was close to nine in the evening. So OK, I stopped in a few places en route.

1. To erase the very chill he'd sunk in me bones.

2. The shock of the developed film had walloped me hard.

The smell hit me first.

Rank,

foul,

dead.

It literally knocked me back into the corridor.

Took a deep breath, gathered me shredded nerves, went in.

The whole apartment was lit up.

Blazing with candles.

Black candles.

Almost fifty at a rough estimate. On every surface.

On the coffee table was a dead dog.

Headless.

Gutted from end to end.

The entrails spilling on to the wooden floor.

Took me a moment to realize there was a note pinned to the poor animal's hind quarters.

A very bloodied note. Read:

'Dog-gone.'

And on the bookcase, a red card – and I mean crimson. With more than a little trepidation, I opened it. It seemed to be some kind of invitation. The words in black read:

Missa niger.
Invito te venire ad clandestinum ritum.

And it was signed, 'The Devil's Minion'.

The acid-thrower, not hiding the fact that he'd re-decorated my apartment. The bastard had balls, I'd give him that, and I swore,

'You'll fucking need them, pal.'

I stood, frozen, as I surveyed my home.

Then rage kicked in. Never underestimate the dark power, the energy of that. It galvanizes you, has you muttering,

'By Jaysus.'

If there is a better antidote to terror, a sawn-off not being to hand, bring it on.

I grabbed the help that was on site.

Xanax,

Jameson,

and a primed and loaded gun.

Whoever had black candled my place hadn't found the gun. It was wrapped in oilskin, under a pile of dirty laundry.

Burglars know that old ploy, but this intruder hadn't come to steal.

Once the weapon was in me hand, I began to feel, if not better, at least less powerless. I gripped it like me first Holy Communion money. Then:

double Jameson (neat),

double Xanax (neater),

and mused on the poor dog's head.

Where would the sick fucker have put it, going for max effect as he was? Godfather like, in me bed?

I'd check that once the meds hit.

The fridge, of course.

On ice, so to speak.

I added another dollop of the Jay, me gut warming already and a ferocious anger building. The magic of prescription drugs, a frigging song began to roll in me head.

Now?

I'm standing in the centre of my apartment, with a head-less dog, its entrails dripping still on to me floor, my system ablaze with whiskey and dope, my temper close to Delcon three, a loaded, primed weapon in my right hand, and I'm humming 'The Boys Are Back In Town'?

Like on auto, this is followed by 'Not A Dry Eye In The House'.

Maybe twenty minutes in, I ease my grip on the weapon. The butt is slick from sweat, my fingers aching from the pressure.

I find my mobile, call Stewart.

Takes a time, but eventually,

'Lo?'

Jesus, now even 'Hello' is abbreviated?

'Stewart, I need your help.'

Pause.

'Er, Jack, this is not like . . . er . . . the best moment.'

Discretion never being me strongest suit and me not being in the best of tempers, I snapped,

'What? It's not like you're getting laid or something.'

Whoops.

He said,

'Actually . . .'

Christ, his date with the freaking vegan lawyer. He was *scoring*?

I could hear muttered whispering.

Pillow talk?

Like I'd know.

He asked,

'Where are you?'

I nearly said, *Iraq, why else would I call*?

Went with,

'Me apartment.'
'OK, I'll be there in, say, twenty.'
Clicked off.
What? No pithy Zen aphorism?

I slunk down against the wall, the bookcase to my right, my eyes locked on the still-open door.

The black candles threw macabre shadows dancing along the ceiling.

The gun was resting on the floor, a Hail Mary from my hand.

If anyone other than Stewart came calling, he'd better have made peace with his maker. It would be a real bad time for the Mormons to be house calling.

I'd never noticed before, but pinned to the side of the bookcase was:

God is in the most secret corner of your life,
Where no one reaches,
Where a voice which comes and goes mysteriously tells you
What you do not want to hear.
Recall what you would prefer to forget
And
What you do not want to know.
He is that profound abyss of
Your unbelief.
He is in that
Which you feel you have lost,
That you fear

You will not find again,
And which you wish to possess,
Although
You would be ashamed
To admit it
To other people.

Fuck, maybe the Mormons had been after all.

I nipped at the Jay to keep me focus sharp, me rage on fire, thought of Serena May and the golden child she'd been. And almost as outrider to her, Lee Ann Womack's 'I Hope You Dance'.

My mind like a cobra, lashing all over the place.

Time moved on. My cocktail of booze and pharmaceuticals had zoned me out. Languidly, I reached to the bookcase. Always wanted to be *languid* as opposed to langers. Using the Dice Man method of random selection, I'd see what spoke to me.

Seamus Smyth, his second great novel, *Red Dock*.

What the nuns did to the poor Magdalen girls, the Christian Brothers did to the boys, in the so termed 'Industrial Schools'. Translate as 'Concentration Camps'.

With total Church approval.

The opening lines had me spitting iron.

Stewart appeared in the doorway and I came as close to shooting him as I don't want to dwell upon.

He was wearing a T-shirt with the logo 'Above the saddle, no rider. Below the saddle, no rider.'

Was he fucking kidding me?

He stared in, disbelief writ neon, muttered in very un-Stewart fashion,

'Holy shite.'

I said languidly,

'Don't be shy, come in. It gets, if not better, a whole lot more interesting.'

He advanced cautiously, as if something was going to bite him.

Well, he was safe enough from the dog, I reckoned.

His eyes remained on my gun till he saw the coffee table, and it looked like he was going to throw up.

Guess Zen didn't cover that.

I asked,

'Any thoughts on where a sick bollix would stash the head?'

He managed to compose himself, asked,

'What the fuck happened?'

In nigh most of the years I'd known him, through

dope-dealer,

convict,

businessman,

Zen pain in the arse,

that's if anyone ever *knew* him,

he never swore.

Perhaps he felt no need, but now he was effing and blinding like the rest of the country. Like a priest counting the takings after Sunday Mass.

I laid out the whole gig, even the pictures that hadn't developed.

He seemed mesmerized by the array of black candles.

When I'd finished, I asked,
'Is there a Zen message to explain this?'
He said,
'Shit happens.'

16

'I smoked too much and had a sore chest. I had a host of companion symptoms as well, niggly physical things that showed up occasionally, weird aches, possible lumps, rashes, symptoms of a condition maybe, or a network of conditions. What if they all held hands one day and lit up?'

Alan Glynn, *The Dark Fields*

We didn't find the head.

I had a horrible feeling it would turn up in the most appalling manner. *Bring Me the Head of Alfredo Garcia*. Where was Warren Oates when you needed him?

I did find the crumpled napkin that Carl had written on. Smoothed it out and read:

1. Sarah Goode.
2. Sarah Osborn.
3. Tibuta.

Handed it to Stewart, said,

'Zen this.'

He went to my laptop, began to Google furiously.

My eyes strayed to the bookcase, to Edward Wright's superb novel, *Damnation Falls*. I thought,

'Ed, buddy, you got that bang to rights.'

Stewart was making odd noises, maybe his mantra. Finally he sat back and said,

'Jack, you'd better take a look at this.'

It showed that on March 1st 1692, those three people were arrested for witchcraft in Salem.

Stewart said,

'The night we went to Ridge's, Carl was smoking some kind of cheroots, but later, I saw him outside, smoking cigarettes.'

I said,

'Fascinating as that is, what the fuck does it have to do with this?'

He gave me that patient look, said,

'He smoked maybe five cigarettes, one after another, and then crumpled the packet and threw it on the ground. You know I hate litter and I went to pick it up.'

Jesus, would he ever get to the frigging point? I said,

'Hooray, you get the Good Citizen of the Month award.'

He ignored that, said,

'Green packet, American . . . Salem's.'

'I've no idea what this means.'

He shrugged, said,

'Except that something seriously weird is happening here.'

'Yah think?'

While he was Googling so well, I handed him the red card, said,

'Track this, genius.'

Didn't take long. He let out a breath, said,

'It's an invitation to a black Mass.'

I asked,

'Any RSVP?'

He closed the laptop, sweat visible on his forehead.

I figured to cut him some slack. Told him he should be getting back to his lady and said,

'Mary . . . how was it?'

'It's Aine, and it was great till you called.'

I apologized and thanked him for coming over.

He nodded, asked,

'What will you do now?'

'Blow out the candles.'

At the door, he cautioned,

'This is very bad karma, Jack. You should walk – no, run away, right now.'

Running has never been me strong point. The limp didn't help.

I bundled the carcass in a bin liner, dropped another Xanax, washed it down with a shot of Jay, put my gun in my Garda coat.

I had a concert to attend.

The Devil's Minions were ending their set when I got to the Roisin Dubh.

The guy who'd acided me was the lead singer, and fucking bad he was.

I knew the barman, pushed a fifty note across to him, said,

'Seamus, tell the lead singer there's some hot babe in the alley panting for him.'

He asked,

'This going to come back on me?'

I let go of the fifty and he took it.

The back of Roisin's borders the canal. Dark and ominous at that hour.

I hadn't long to wait.

The side door opened and he emerged, the sweat on his face gleaming in the dim streetlight, his gig or the promise of a blow job lighting him up.

I shot him in both knees, from behind, then caught him as he fell, picked him up and threw him in the canal.

I hefted the bin liner, threw it in too.

Like the very last lines of *Under the Volcano*. They'd thrown a dead dog into a hole after the consul's body. It gave, I felt, a nice literary touch to the proceedings.

On my way home, I found a phone box that hadn't been vandalized.

Rang the Guards, said a man was drowning in the canal.

I didn't mention the dog.

He'd had his day.

Next day, I went to see the tinkers.

Once treated as the dregs of our caring society, they'd moved up a notch since we started to resent the non-nationals. Not a huge leap for them, but they were getting less abuse than before.

I'd worked a case with and for them, and thus was regarded as close to clan as an outsider is ever going to get.

As a child, I remember, every Monday the skin woman would come, collecting discarded potato skins to feed her pigs.

Little did she know, the fucking skins were our dinner

most days.

She did this for years.

After her death, it was disclosed that she never had any pigs.

I went to see her sister, Peg, who it was claimed had the gift of *the sight*. Yeah, I know, HBO already have the series. Before *Ghost Whisperer*, *Crossing Over*, *Sixth Sense*, before all that, she was quietly dispensing such things as she intuited.

Her caravan was perched on the football field in the Claddagh.

Recently, asbestos had been discovered there and house prices had plummeted.

Guess she didn't see *that* coming.

But I was clutching at straws.

She lived alone and, unusual for a traveller, not a dog in sight, or even a pig.

I came prepared.

Bottle of Jameson,

dozen cans of Guinness,

carton of cigs, and at nigh ten Euro a pack, I was hurting.

Plus a fresh salmon I'd bought from one of the local 'snatchers'. How fresh was it going to be from our now perennially poisoned water?

I knocked on her door, on the Evil Eye symbol where most people would have their spy hole.

She opened the door slowly. If you're a tinker, you always answer slowly. Stared at me, said,

'Jack Taylor.'

I handed over the booty/bribe, said,

'I need a reading, Peg *a gra*.'

She waved me in.

A tall woman, had to be near eighty now, her hair neatly styled, and those piercing blue eyes, cataracts forming but not dulling the sheer intensity. She had that regal bearing some women achieve no matter what shite comes down the road.

Wearing a Connemara shawl, the real deal, hand sewn and passed from one generation to another.

Long skirt that swished as she moved.

Her sole jewellery was a miraculous medal, gold of course.

The caravan was spotless, and devoid of furniture save for two hard-backed chairs, one wooden table and a narrow bed, neatly made.

Zen, in fact.

Like most of her generation, she switched from Irish to English at will. Like the song goes,

> and speak a language
> that the foreigner does not know.

We sat, she opened the Jay, poured liberal amounts in heavy Galway crystal tumblers, toasted,

'*Dia agus a Mhathair leat.*' (God and His Holy Mother with you.)

I said,

'*Leat fein.*' (You too.)

The neat Jay burned like false hope.

She cracked two cans of the Guinness, pushed one across.

'*Ta an doireachdeas leat.*' (The darkness is upon you.)

No fucking around, then.

I told her the whole story.

She never interrupted, just sipped from the Guinness, her eyes glued to my face.

Finished, I sat back, knackered, and took a long swig from the Jay.

She asked,

'Did you take money from him?'

Fuck.

Tricky ground.

I scratched the card he sent me, won the big one, but I could easily have lost . . . right?

Didn't fly.

If I lied to her once, I was history.

I told her.

She nodded, said,

'He owns yer arse.'

I asked,

'What will I do?'

She reached behind her for a pack of Sweet Afton.

They still made those suckers?

My dad used to smoke them.

Lord rest him.

I remembered the lines of the Scottish poet Burns on the front.

Reading me expression, she said,

'*Deanamh caitheamh tobac dubthal thremous leat.*'

Sounds freaking ominous, right?

It's the current government warning on packs and tells you that terrible things will happen to you if you smoke.

Next, she produced an old box of Swan matches, offered both to me.

Rough.

I hadn't smoked for three years.

Fucking quitting was just one of the many afflictions I've endured.

But to refuse?

Couldn't.

Bollix.

I took two out, handed her one, fired us up.

The smell of sulphur was like a bad joke.

Coarse, no filters on these babies.

The real deal.

She took a deep drag.

Me too.

Christ Almighty, they kicked like a demented Guard on late-Saturday-night drunk tank.

Her face, impossibly lined, seemed to suck into itself.

My first inhalation had me dizzy.

Delicious lethal delight.

In answer, finally, as to what I should do, she said,

'*Rith*.' (Run.)

Took me a moment to catch the twinkle in her eye.

She asked,

'Do you believe in the Devil?'

'I believe.'

She extended her palm and it took me a moment to catch up.

Cross her hand with silver.

Like all the shite I'd paid a fortune for wasn't enough?

I found a two Euro coin, not silver but jeez, who was keeping count? I placed it dead centre in her palm and she closed her hand, intoned,

'*Uber,*

ubris,

iosa.'

A lot of other stuff I didn't grasp, seemed a blend of Irish and Latin.

She commanded,

'On your knees.'

I did as she told me.

She rose, stood over me, then pulled a small phial from her pocket and began to sprinkle it over me. Said,

'Holy water.'

Or poison.

Who knew?

She said another long prayer and my leg was acting up. Eventually, she took a leather thong, a miraculous medal attached, hung it round my neck and said,

'*Mhathair an Iosa leat.*' (God's Mother be with you.)

Unless the Madonna was packing serious heat, I felt I was fucked.

She motioned me to rise. We were done.

I had an envelope ready, laid it on the table.

She said,

'Thanks, son.'

She poured us both a farewell Jay, asked,

'Can you kill a man?'

She knew my history, what I had done in the past for the clans, but this was a different dance.

I said I could.

She muttered,

'*Ta tu an bronach nach bhfuail feidire leat a rith.*'

Literally, it means you are the kind of person who is not able to run, but it has *bronach* in there which gives a whole other dimension, meaning what a sadness, you aren't the type to quit.

I wanted to shout, *I would if I could, but I can't.*

But she already knew that.

We were done, and to my astonishment she hugged me.

Blame the damn cigarettes, but I felt me eyes well up.

As I headed for the door, her parting line was,

'*Is anois an t'amall an fear seo a marbh.*'

There are various translations for this, but in a nutshell it means,

'Kill him now.'

17

'The Devil plays with a loaded deck.'

Old Irish proverb

After Taylor left, Peg said a small Novena for him. Like all the tinkers, she had a deep love for the man.

All those years ago, when young tinkers were being slaughtered, their bodies thrown in the fair green, did the Guards help?

She gave a bitter laugh.

Did they shite.

The Garda Suichona . . . Guardians of the Peace.

Her arse they were.

More like Garda Chickana.

That Superintendent . . . Clancy?

Oh, a bad bastard.

Was overheard on the golf course saying,

'Good riddance to bad rubbish.'

This was, of course, off the record, a private remark if you will.

In Ireland, a 'private remark' is like putting it on a billboard.

Then along came the bedraggled, befuddled Taylor, a broken man to hear it said. And 'fond of it'.

Meaning, a drunk.

Taylor was wounded in all the ways that last. He took up their cause. And took some serious beatings along the way. One horrendous one, they literally kicked the teeth out of his head. Beat him with the ash, the hurleys giving him that limp.

Did he run?

She smiled. He kept on coming. Like a dog who will not quit, no matter how many times you wallop it. She blessed herself for him and her own self. He had solved the case.

Above all, he had true respect and affection for the clans. They never forget and he was among the few outsiders to be considered almost one of their own.

She poured a large Jay, raised it and said aloud,

'*Bhi curamach*.' (Be careful.)

She felt the Jameson light her stomach, like the child she'd never have. A wave of weariness began to wash over her. Maybe she'd just rest her eyes for a wee while.

Her dreams were vivid. She saw Taylor so clearly, going willingly towards a man. She wanted to cry,

'No, not the Lord of Lies, he believes he owns you.'

The rest of the dream involved fire and a cemetery of young people.

She woke with a small sigh.

Her body was covered in sweat and yet she was frozen, ice cold.

But she'd left the heaters on, she could have sworn.

Then she saw the man sitting at the table. Long golden

hair, like her Lord, Jesus. The same golden tresses as in the huge portrait of the Sacred Heart she prized.

Till he turned.

Looked at her.

Eyes . . . of yellow?

And a beautiful suit.

She had seen such clothes in the shops on the main street that would never let the likes of her inside.

He gave a smile of such radiance, her hopes rose briefly, till he spoke.

'Peg, I thought you were sleeping the sleep of the damned.'

And he laughed.

A sound that sent slivers of ice along her spine. He lifted the miraculously full Jameson bottle, poured two generous glasses, said,

'Come, drink with me.'

As if mesmerized, she rose, moved slowly to the table and took the hard chair.

His eyes were locked on hers.

She prayed she was still dreaming and somehow she'd wake.

Safe.

Warm.

He pushed the glass towards her, raised his own, asked,

'Peg, oh Peg, my heart, what shall we drink to?'

She grabbed the glass, like some futile lifeline, drained half, seeking heat and oblivion.

He said,

'I know, let's drink to Jack Taylor.'

A beat. Then,

'That work for you, Peg? A toast to the bold Jack?'

Each time he uttered her name, it was like a laceration on her soul. He indicated the ashtray. Two cigarettes, newly lit, were waiting.

She knew she was done for, but damned, by God, never that.

As she took the cigarette, he said,

'All your needs are catered for, Peg.'

Her hand trembled and he watched it, said,

'Woe is me, if only this whole episode were just the jigs, as you Irish call them. How amusing that your favourite dance is also what you call the horrors, Deliria Tremens. You could deal with that Peg, right? *C'est vrai?*'

She stared at him, defiance writ large.

He laughed, said,

'*Excusez-moi*, what would a peasant like you know of such a language as French?'

She finally found her voice, fingering the gold miraculous medal round her neck, said,

'What do you want?'

He lunged across the table, tore the medal from her neck and flung it across the caravan.

'You think such trifles can help you?'

She was shocked. The touch of his hand was like a knife wound, and cold, like a dead heart. Her heart pounded but she managed,

'You have no business with me.'

He laughed anew, but in a new tenor, pure unadulterated malevolence, said,

'You told Mr Taylor that he was tainted, that he had taken the Devil's coin?'

Peg was of pure tinker stock, she'd known every humiliation the world could cast. She had fronted up to bailiffs, sheriffs, Guards, tormentors of every sort, and had never given one inch.

But now?

Now she was terrified.

He indicated the booze, the cigarettes, said,

'Purchased with . . . how should I put it? The same currency.'

She had to know, asked,

'Why are you so focused on one wreck of a man, a poor creature who is only of danger to his own self?'

His lips drew back and she'd have sworn he snarled, but he reined it in. He lifted the box of matches slowly, methodically. Lighting them, flicking them across the table, on the floor, he said,

'Very eloquently spoken, for a . . .'

The curtains caught fire, a bundle of *Galway Advertisers*, a flier for takeaway pizza.

'. . . A barren sow.'

He filled her glass as the smoke began to envelop them, said,

'I'm a very busy man – swine flu, genocide, the usual manifestations of my power, mild diversions if you will. But I do have certain fetishes, some idle projects I like to see come to fruition. A mere drop in the ocean, but of amusement to me.'

Then he was on his feet, towering over her. His voice like the awesome storm of '82, he boomed,

'And I will not be thwarted. These *diversions* have their place and are of some value to me.'

The smoke was hurting her eyes, invading her lungs, but she was transfixed. He continued,

'Some years ago, I had wonderful aspirations for a young man, a true believer, and he was doing so well, laying waste to the young of your tribe, who even your own nation despises.'

Despite the fire raging, the congestion in her lungs, she managed to smile, said,

'And Jack Taylor stepped in.'

His blow knocked her from the chair and sent her sprawling close to the burning curtains. He strode over, said,

'Cunt, listen well, he has meddled many times. I even had a nun turned. Have you any idea, in your tinker's soul, what it means to own a nun, what a spit in the face of the Nazarene that would have been, a Bride of Christ doing my unholy work?'

She would never know how she managed it, but she laughed, laughed at him, said,

'And Jack stopped her, didn't he? Despite all your fireworks and scare tricks, this small, insignificant man yet again kicked you in the balls, which I doubt you have. You might be the Lord of Hell, but it takes no balls to hit a woman. It takes a long yellow streak, as yellow as your piss-tinted eyes.'

He grabbed her hair, pushed her face into the flaming newspapers, said,

'You will kneel before me, or by the Christ you worship, you will die a death you never imagined.'

She somehow dredged up a mere dribble of spit, spat it on his beautiful trousers, cried,

'You're a poor excuse for a devil, God help us, and mark my words, you cowardly piece of shite, Jack Taylor will show you hell before you're through.'

True to his word, he made her die hard.

Very.

But kneel?

Never.

The caravan burned quickly. By the time the fire brigade arrived, it was but a smouldering shell.

One of the firemen, moving towards the debris, spotted a glint, reached down and picked out a medal. He held it up to the light. For years after, he'd swear 'It shone like the purest gold.'

A passer-by said to his mate,

'Another dead tinker, what a fucking surprise.'

On Long Walk, across the water from the caravan, the man with the golden tresses fumed, said,

'Taylor, she goes on your list. The sow never knelt, but you will.'

The sun lit up the ruined caravan and the burnt remains of Peg.

The man knew that what her charred remains might yield was a smile of pure victory.

As he stomped along Long Walk, even the swans withdrew from his passing, huddled on the other shore.

Despite the sun's brief respite, he threw no shadow.

18

'Lie with your eyes, your mouth will follow their lead.'

KB

I heard about the fire on the radio. Jimmy Norman's show. He'd been playing one of me all-time favourites, Nilsson's 'If Living Is Without You'.

That he died of booze endeared him to me anyway, but this song reminded me of when I'd met the love of me life and she left me for a Guard, because, she said,

'You're a hopeless drunk.'

Yeah, I know, it's a classic whine-into-your-glass dirge, but no less effective for that.

Time eases all pain.

What a fucking crock.

Sometimes I thought I saw her on the street and me heart died all over again.

I nearly missed the news item.

As it sunk in, I wanted to weep. The fire department believed the woman had fallen asleep with a burning cigarette in her hand.

The inference being 'a drunk'.

An empty whiskey bottle found amid the charred remains seemed to endorse their premiss.

Like the Peter Gabriel song, I grieved, in ribbons over her terrible death, song titles mutating like wrapped cobras in me fevered brain.

I muttered Leonard Cohen's 'Who By Fire?'.

Why the fuck did I bring booze and cigarettes to her?

I didn't know if I could go to the funeral. Tinkers grieve like Muslim women, the awful keening and wailing. I wasn't sure my shredded nerves could withstand it.

But Jesus, I could do flowers, had to.

Rang Interflora.

The woman was sympathetic without being cloying.

I ordered a dozen red roses and she asked if I'd like to add a note. I said, 'Just "Deepest condolences, Jack Taylor".'

A pause and I figured she was writing it down, then she asked,

'You live at Nun's Island?'

'Yes.'

'So you wish to send a second wreath?'

'What?'

'Bear with me a moment, Mr Taylor. I haven't been in the office for the past few days, touch of flu, and the girl I have, not a fecking clue, just boys, boys, boys.'

I needed to hear about her personal fucking problems? I gave a snort of impatience. She caught it, said as she shuffled through papers,

'This is very odd.'

'What?'

She sounded almost panicked.

'Must be that nitwit of a girl. According to the dates, the wreath was ordered . . . the day before the poor unfortunate woman died.'

I felt a wave of dizziness, but asked,

'What does the card say?'

'I beg your pardon?'

Now she was getting attitude?

'The card for the first wreath?'

'But Mr Taylor, you wrote it, didn't you?'

Christ on a bike. I said,

'Please forgive me, but grief, it has me all over the place.'

She eased a notch, said,

'Of course, Mr Taylor, I empathize.'

I prompted,

'The card?'

'Oh, of course, it reads . . . well, it seems a touch odd.'

I waited.

'It reads . . . "Didn't *see* this coming."'

I hung up.

See.

It wasn't possible, couldn't be. I tried to get my mind into focus. The note could only be from one source.

I asked myself for the hundredth time,

'What does the Devil want with me?'

The old people used to say,

'The Devil can only enter your life if you invite him.'

Had I?

In my darkest hours, I'd ranted and sworn at God.

Hunched over a toilet bowl, puking me guts out, I remember I'd cried,

'Anyone else out there?'

Never, never thinking there was a darkness waiting to be bidden.

I'd lived in the dark so long.

Had the darkness come to live in me?

I muttered,

'Jesus, Mary and Joseph.'

I had to get out, walk the town, dispel the shadows. The pelting rain had eased but I grabbed my all-weather coat. The Sig fitted neatly in the right pocket. Popped the Xanax and headed out. Something about the date was itching at me subconscious.

A newspaper confirmed my unease. The tenth anniversary of Columbine. Whatever you believed, the Devil had stalked the halls of the high school that awful day.

Coincidence?

They say coincidence is when God wishes to appear anonymous.

He was sure keeping one blitz of a low profile these days.

And the other gem,

'If God seems far away, who moved?'

Bollix.

I walked down Shop Street. A mime artist dressed as the Joker was performing outside Garavan's. I dropped some coins in his box and he said,

'Joke's on you, boyo.'

My temper was not at its best, the Xanax was failing to chill me. I snapped, asked,

'Aren't you fuckers supposed to be silent or did I miss something?'

He smiled, and I hoped those yellow fangs were part of the make-up. He said,

'You missed the bigger picture.'

It wouldn't look too great if I was to be seen beating the living be-jaysus out of a street performer.

I moved on.

At Anthony Ryan's, the clothes shop, a figure emerged, bustling with bags of stuff. Stopped and lit a cigarette.

Who else?

The nicotine czar, his own self, Father Malachy.

I said,

'Business must be good if you can shop in Ryan's.'

He looked terrible.

Christ, he always looked woebegone but now he had an added air of desperation. The ubiquitous dandruff lined the black shoulders of his suit. He hadn't shaved and the grey stubble gave him the aura of a dank wino. His hair was like a bedraggled crow.

He neither heard nor saw me. I moved closer and a shower had been least of his priorities, it seemed. I asked,

'They give you a clerical discount there?'

His eyes finally registered and he stared at me . . . in relief?

He took me completely out of left field, grabbed my arm, said,

'Let's get a jar.'

All the years he'd torn me limb from fragile limb over my drinking, and now this? I was about to say,

'Never look a gift priest in the mouth.'

But he looked too close to the brink, so I said,

'Sure, you're paying, so yeah.'

We went to Feeney's, close to where Kenny's wondrous bookshop used to be located. It was that rarity, unchanged. Not too far from the old pawn shop, where my late mother used to hock my dad's suit and his beloved pocket watch.

She had hocked his life a long time before that.

Years ago, when I drank in Grogan's, and had my loved friends, Jeff and Cathy, and their golden child, Serena May . . .

But I can't dwell on them or the child.

Two sentries held up either end of the bar there. Two old men in cloth caps, always nourishing a half-full/empty pint, and as far as I knew they never spoke to each other.

But they were as reliable as a sincere prayer.

All the bad shite that had ensued over the years, I'd lost track of them. I'd presumed, hoped, they still kept their vigil there. And even though Grogan's had been sold after the death of the child, I clung to the hope that they had found stools in some other old Galway bar.

As we entered Feeney's, right by the door was one of them.

I realized I never knew their names. So I did the Irish dance, asked,

'How've you been?'

He looked at me and the same disinterest he'd always shown was still alive. He said,

'Middling.'

That's as close to 'Fuck off' as it gets.

But I persisted, asked,

'And, er . . . your friend?'

'He wasn't my friend.'

I began to move off, wasn't going to do a whole lot of spreading the joy there, and he said,

'He died.'

I nodded, kept going.

I'd read my Russell Friedman on grief and how not to express remorse/sorrow for someone you never knew.

Some books do actually help.

My sympathy would only have elicited more bitterness and I'd enough of my own to be going on with.

Malachy had gone right down to the end of the pub and found a table, and I joined him. I figured he'd already put in an order.

Sure enough, the drinks came.

Two large Jamesons.

No ice.

The barman said,

'On the house, Father.'

If Malachy was grateful, he was hiding it. He said, 'I don't see you at Mass.'

The barman gave him a look – not of respect or awe, those days were well over – said,

'I took my business elsewhere.'

And moved off.

Malachy, already raising his glass, muttered,

'A pup, that fellah.'

Not a compliment. I raised my glass, toasted,

'Good health.'

He made a sound halfway between *hmmph* and *Is it on meself?* Then drained most of the double Jay.

I did the same.

Waited.

The whiskey hit him fast, a crimson glow mounting like sunburn up his cheeks, making his battered face almost glow. He said,

'I don't have many friends in the priesthood.'

I was surprised he had any friends anywhere, but kept my mouth shut. He continued,

'Over in the Claddagh, Father Ralph was my friend. We were in Maynooth together and took our final vows on the same day. We always stayed in touch, a card or letter, even after he went on the Missions.'

I had no idea where this was going.

Something between a sigh and groan escaped him as he said,

'I can't believe he's dead.'

Took me a moment, then I blurted,

'Ralph's dead?'

He was startled, turned to look at me.

'You knew him?'

I was trying to focus, muttered,

'I met him once. I liked him a lot.'

Malachy shook his head, amazed and, I think, angry. I'd known his friend. Then he made that condescending gesture that serious drinkers all over the fucking world hate. He raised his hand in a drinking gesture to his mouth, the words conveying, in bright shame, *alkie*. Said, as if I didn't get it already,

'Fond of it, you know, no denying that. But to do what he did, I never realized he was so far gone.'

Had I missed something? I was trying so hard not to lash him across his smug non-*alkie* face that rage temporarily blinded me. I asked,

'What did he do?'

Jesus wept. Not another child molester. That I couldn't stomach, not now. Malachy said,

'Your turn for a round, I believe.'

The bollix.

I jumped up, went to the counter, tried to rein in the ferocious wave building, said to the barman,

'Same again, please,'

and put a twenty Euro note on the counter lest he think I was freeloading.

If he thought neat larges that early in the day were odd, he said nothing. He got the drinks, gave me the pittance change, said, nodding to Malachy,

'Contrary bastard.'

I took the drinks, looked at the paltry change, said,

'Put it in the Missions box.'

He laughed, said,

'Where have you been? We are the Missions.'

I got back to the table – no sign of Malachy. I looked round and the barman indicated the shed beside the bar.

The smokers' room.

Beside the toilets, of course.

I sat, sipping my fresh drink, trying to keep my mind blank and a lid on my temper.

Malachy returned, reeking of cigarettes, sat, grabbed the new drink and downed a fair portion. Then took a breath and said,

'They've covered it up, of course, said he died of a heart attack. If the truth came out, they'd be more banjaxed than before.'

He emitted a long sad sigh, said,

'He hanged himself.'

I was appalled, said,

'I'm so sorry.'

He rounded on me, spittle dribbling from the corners of his mouth, accused,

'*You?* You're sorry? I thought the likes of you would dance a jig at the clergy being destroyed.'

I understood the blind lashing out of grief, had done it often enough, and when you add Jameson to a simmering fire . . . I said,

'You make me sound like the Devil.'

He sat back, drained instantly, said,

'I met a man last week, he frightened me, Jack.'

Jack!

'Good-looking fellah, lovely suit, said he wanted to make

a donation to the Church fund and asked me to excuse his poor English. I think he was French, said he'd been recommended by you! At first I was glad – we're always happy with donations and supporters of the Church – till he began to look at me. He scared me, Jack. It was like he was – Jesus, God forgive me for taking the Holy Name in vain, but he looked like pure badness, and as he was leaving, he handed me a large wad of notes – hundred notes they were, Jack – and said with this awful smile . . .'

He had to stop. Sweat was pouring down his face and he grabbed at his glass, then continued,

'He said, "Priests shouldn't be hanging round." Jack, he stressed hanging, and as he left, he stopped and said, "If you really are a friend of our Jack, I might have to return, make another *donation*." '

I didn't like Malachy, never had, but I didn't like to see him afraid. I asked,

'Who do you think he was?'

He jumped up, his eyes mad in his head, shouted,

'You're the Devil's spawn! Even your blessed mother, God rest her, she always said some day he'd come to claim you.'

And he stormed out.

I finished my drink and thought, if I was going to hell, the worst thing would be that the bitch she'd been all her miserable life was sure to be the first to welcome me.

Ian Dury and the Blockheads – the cheerful face of punk, if there was such a thing – had a big hit with 'Reasons To Be Cheerful'.

For the life of me, I couldn't think of one.

Ian Dury, badly crippled by polio as a child, never gave anything but his best in concert.

He had passed on too.

Everybody of fucking note had.

I finished my drink, headed out and said to the lone sentry,

'God mind you well.'

He never looked up from his pint, said,

'God, like the rest of the slick bastards, moved to a tax haven.'

What to say?

Save think of what Ronnie Scott said to Van Morrison,

'You've made a happy man very old.'

19

'And then he assigns you his sacred fire, that you may become sacred bread for God's sacred feast.'

Khalil Gibran, *The Prophet*

My limp had been acting up and I figured a decent walk might ease the ache. I took the route that leads to Grattan Road. But first I went to the Dominican church, to see Our Lady of Galway. When I'd sheltered from the rain and met Father Ralph I'd never given her a second thought, so if I made up for the lapse now, who knew, maybe she'd appreciate it.

A seventeenth-century Italian Madonna. There is a mother-of-pearl bead in her hand, given by a fisherman.

Her crown was presented by the first ever Catholic mayor of Galway in 1683.

She was literally buried when the waves of persecution began.

I love the altar surrounding her, it shows

a Claddagh boat,

St Nicholas, patron saint of Galway,

St Enda, venerated on the Aran Islands.

It is said that if a real Galwegian asks her help, she will grant it.

So I asked,

'What am I supposed to do?'

Waited, then decided that walking was the only thing I was able to do just now. I blessed myself, then headed on, moved along Grattan Road, glancing to the right at the abandoned lighthouse. Maybe I could rent that and put the isolation in its proper place. I reached the aquarium. I'd never been inside. Perhaps they had displays of the poisoned water.

Beside it was Seapoint ballroom. My mind attempted to recapture those glory days of the showbands:

The Regal,

The Capitol,

The Clipper Carlton,

The Indians,

The Royal,

The Miami.

Dressed in blazers and pants with actual creases, those guys played three-hour sessions, and the crowd loved them. I'm not going into some rap about a more innocent time, but the fact we knew less seemed to suit us better.

Now we know everything and talk to nobody.

A priest would patrol outside to ensure lewd behaviour didn't occur. If only we knew, we should have been patrolling the priests.

As I hit the promenade proper, I gazed out at the ocean. It never failed to make me yearn. For what?

America,

love,

peace?

I don't know, but it was like balm to my tired soul. It didn't quiet the voices in my head that had the same refrain of

reminding,

re-telling,

reprimanding

the trash I was.

Once a cop . . .

Those instincts never fully leave you.

I'd been aware for the past ten minutes of a sleek black BMW tracking me.

Sawyer's men?

Payback?

The Sig was to hand. I was ready and be-jaysus, I was willing.

I kept walking, replaying my most recent conversation with Stewart, his anger at my insistence that we were dealing with the Devil. He even asked if I'd checked for the number 666. I'd laughed out loud, said,

'He's bald, how hard would it be to look?'

Then I added, venom spilling all over my words,

'You saw *The Omen* and bought the glitz version.'

He didn't know what I meant so I told him.

Hollywood versus Revelation.

And read out the actual passage from Revelation, 13, 16–18:

'And he causeth all, both small and great, rich and poor, free and bond, to receive a mark in their right hand, or in their

foreheads. And that no man might buy or sell, save he that had the mark, or the name of the beast, or the number of his name. Here is wisdom. Let him that hath understanding count the number of the beast: for it is the number of a man; and his number is six hundred three score and six.'

He was confused and I said,

'The number 666 is the mark of the beast, not of Satan!'

The BMW stopped, the back door opened and a voice said,

'Get in.'

Cautiously I bent down and there was Superintendent Clancy. Once my best friend, but my lethal adversary for a long time. In my last case, I had saved the life of his child and he owed me. I knew he hated that, the debt. I got in, closed the door. Sitting in the front were two Guards, plain clothes. One I didn't know, but the other, he had beaten me to a pulp the year before. He was known as Tom the Thug. It fitted. I said,

'How's the hurting biz, Tommy?'

He didn't reply, but I could see his neck redden from temper.

Clancy said,

'Always with the mouth, Jack?'

Jack.

For years, it had always been Taylor.

I looked at him. He was in full regalia, the deep-navy Commander's rig, with medals pinned on the right collar. He'd been carrying a lot of weight the last time we met, but seemed to have grown even larger, his stomach pressed against the tight tunic. His jowls testified to rich dinners with the lads and layers of fat had narrowed his eyes into slits. I asked,

'Life treating you good?'

He sighed and I knew he was waiting for me to ask about the boy, to remind him.

I didn't.

He said,

'I was reliably informed you were going to America.'

I smiled, said,

'Not that reliable, it seems.'

Usually, at this stage in the proceedings, one of his men would have walloped me, hard. He said,

'Jack, we have the Volvo racing competition coming to Galway. Out of all the cities in the world, we get to be the base. This means a huge influx of money, prestige, tourists, puts us on the world stage.'

He paused, shot his hand out, adjusted the cufflink on his snow-white shirt.

Who the fuck wears cufflinks any more and more to the point, why?

I swear, they had the Garda crest on them.

I had a real hard time not to burst into Rod Stewart's 'Sailing', but that would have definitely gotten me a hammering. He continued,

'Now Jack, how would it sound to the world media if some eejit were running round making wild accusations about Satanic murders and such crazy talk as that?'

I said,

'I'm guessing the Tourist Board wouldn't be happy with such an individual.'

He turned his beady eyes on me, said,

'You've got it arseways as usual, Jack. You're forever bleating about not liking our new Galway but it's the other way round, Galway doesn't like you, I don't like you and the fucking Tourist Board is prepared to ship you out themselves.'

Tom laughed out loud, nudged his mate and they snickered in unison. Clancy said,

'Get the fuck out of town, and this warning as opposed to other . . . measures . . . means our slate is clean, am I clear?'

'Yes, sir.'

He made a bone-breaking noise with his fingers, said,

'Get the hell out of my car and remember, next time I'll send Tom alone.'

I was not fully out of the car when the driver put it in gear and roared off. I fell on to the pavement, shouted like the show bands always did,

'Goodnight and God bless.'

I suppose in the interests of truth I'd have to admit that I'd been to see Sawyer but had been holding off on recounting it. I'm not ashamed of it, it needed to be done, but the stuff about his daughters, spoilt or otherwise, made me hesitate to relate the event, the reason why I'd expected Sawyer and not Clancy in that sleek BMW.

In truth, it comes to the same deal.

Thugs and bullies.

Save one wore a uniform.

It was almost too easy to get to him.

Arrogance breeds stupidity and he had both.

In buckets.

He'd played his usual round of golf, seemed mightily pleased with his own self. Had the customary drink with his buddies after, picked up the tab.

Just one of the guys, and generous with it.

Except he kicked the living shite out of a Ban Garda.

My Ban Garda.

Dressed in a cashmere sweater and, I swear to God, a cravat and pleated golfing pants, he was whistling as he headed for his car.

All was hunky fucking dory in this cat's world.

Looked momentarily puzzled as his driver didn't bounce to open the car door.

The driver was out cold in the back seat.

I came up behind Sawyer, smashed his face into the door, broke the fingers of his right hand, the gun nuzzled against the base of his neck, and said in a whisper,

'Once, only once am I going to give you this message.'

Paused.

'Your three spoilt brats of daughters bully a child again,'

I pushed the barrel of the gun harder into his neck,

'I will kill you, your wife, and then I'll take a decent look at your three precious darlings.'

Then I cold-cocked the sucker and got the fuck out of there.

Who says golf chills you out?

The papers reported the Sawyer shooting, the consensus being 'drug related'.

Ireland today had so many drug shootings, even the old reliable drive-by gig didn't warrant the front page any more.

The Cheltenham Race Festival had begun and fears of the recession affecting the number of Irish who usually travelled over to it seemed unfounded.

To the great relief of the Brits.

The Paddy pound, as they termed it, meant a huge source of income to the tiny English town.

They didn't like us any better, but they sure as hell were glad of the Irish insane gambling spirit.

It wasn't just the betting, the Irish liked to party and their parties were the stuff of myth.

Like the Oscars on meth and Jameson.

Publicity wise, Sawyer got shot the wrong week.

The lead singer of the Devil's Minions, nobody gave – forgive the pun – a toss. Trash was tossed in the canal every night.

Sawyer had, to stay with the racing terminology, form.

Or as the Americans say,

'He was a person of interest.'

Did I feel any remorse?

Did I fuck.

Ridge phoned me a few days after, asked if we could meet for a coffee.

I asked if I had to gear up.

She thought I meant clothes.

We met in Café du Journal on Quay Street.

Does it get more Irish?

The place was packed and we had to wait for ten minutes to get a table.

Recession?

Not for the designer-coffee crew, or maybe the news hadn't *filtered* down yet.

Or perhaps, following the government's lead, they just didn't give a fuck.

St Patrick's Day was looming and the government, in the midst of the worst crisis we had faced in twenty years, awarded themselves a twelve-day holiday.

St Patrick had obviously seriously screwed up the ridding-of-snakes gig.

Ridge looked well.

Despite her recent beating, she had an almost healthy glow. Make-up had disguised most of the fading bruises. She was dressed in a tweed suit, as befits the wife of a Lord.

I could see black shadows under her eyes though.

No make-up is that effective.

I know shadows, and not just beneath my eyes.

I lied, said,

'You look great.'

She lied right back.

'You too.'

Getting a table finally near the door, we ordered lattes from the extremely affable Polish waitress. Ridge declined a Danish and me, of course, I don't do sweet.

Never one to preamble, she launched in with,

'I see Mr Sawyer had some bother.'

One way of putting it, I suppose.

I nodded.

She knew, let a silence build, then,

'Thanks.'

I gave her my fake smile, admitting nothing. She was still a Guard.

The coffee came, lots of froth. I asked the waitress,

'Think you could hit that with a double espresso?'

Gave me the radiant smile of another caffeine fiend, said,

'I think we could manage that.'

Ridge sipped at hers, I just knew she couldn't let it slide, said,

'Always the *rush*.'

I could play, went,

'Don't tell me, the movie with Jason Patric and Jennifer Jason Leigh. Not a lot of people know this, but Pete Dexter did the screenplay.'

Movie buffs like that kind of small print.

Ridge didn't.

I think the last movie she saw was *The Quiet Man*.

But Jesus, she'd had the crap beaten out of her by a thug, so I said,

'The rush, the edginess, it's what I'm used to.'

Surprise, surprise, she let it go, asked,

'How was your dinner with Carl?'

I had a lot of answers that didn't contain civility, so I said,

'Didn't develop along the lines I'd anticipated. He speaks very highly of you, though.'

Her face darkened, like a cloud crept behind her eyes and lodged there. She asked,

'Can I be honest?'

It would have been cheap to take a cheap shot. I took it, said,

'Isn't that part of your job description?'

Wounded her and she looked away. I said,

'Tell me.'

She was torn between walloping me and fear. Never an easy choice. She began,

'Anthony has money problems. He had to sell the horses and those thoroughbreds will go to the knacker's yard. He had to sell some land too. The upkeep on the estate is ferocious, we even had to let three of the staff go.'

My heart bled.

Sell the horses?

Let the staff go?

Most of the frigging country couldn't put fuel in their lighters, never mind their cars.

She faltered for a moment then reached in her purse, took out a small gold box. Flipped it like a pro, took out a pill and swallowed it, washing it down with the latte.

I had but a fleeting glimpse of the pill but I know me pharmaceuticals.

Valium 10.

Not yer 5, yer 10.

Mother's little helper.

I didn't comment, waited while she let the Val do its work, weave its artificial magic.

My serious coffee arrived and I took a serious slug of it.

Bliss.

Had instant heart palpitations.

Lock and load.

I thought of me Sig, nestled in the waistband of me jeans.

Never leave home without one.

Mine was the grown-up model, 226. Recently revised to carry fifteen rounds of 9mm Parabellum ammo.

You get what you pay for.

Like the militants' new promise, maybe?

She finally continued and I had to put aside childish things.

Her eyes had that V-glow which delights

Roche,

Bayer,

and all the other legal dope moguls.

She continued,

'Carl showed up, he has such magnificent plans for the estate and he is, as you know, so charming.'

I stayed quiet, thinking,

Charming?

'He seemed the answer to our prayers.'

Made you wonder who they prayed to.

'We were so relieved. Jennifer, Anthony's daughter, would be able to keep her pony and so naturally we invited him to stay with us.'

She took a hit of the latte, maybe the Val gave it a blast, went on,

'Carl liked you so much, Jack, said he could get you into America, and I was so delighted.'

Being the renowned PI I am, I asked,

'And?'

She looked truly scared now, then said,

'It was a few days after the dinner party. I was tidying up. That makes Anthony cross, he says that is the duty of the help, but I suppose you can't escape your upbringing.'

I was wondering how she'd feel about sharing some of the Val. She said,

'I had some fresh towels for Carl. I thought he'd gone shooting with Anthony. They like to get an early start while the pheasants are resting.'

No doubt a peasant would suffice if the birds had flown the coop. She went on,

'I entered his room and he was there. Stark naked.'

Not an image I wanted to cling to. She asked,

'You know how bald he is?'

I thought it depended where and when you met him. Then, she seemed to physically shrink, said,

'He was combing long blond golden hair. I thought it was a wig. I was so shocked, I dropped the towels.'

She squeezed her eyes tight shut for a moment, then said,

'He turned, smiled at me, asked, "Would you like to touch it?"'

Her voice now a little stronger, she said,

'I thought he meant his hair, till I saw . . . Mother of my heart, his . . . phallus. Erect and monstrous.'

She buried her face in her hands, weeping softly. I reached over, took her hands, said,

'It's OK. I know who he is.'

That seemed to help her, and worse, she was grateful. She said,

'Jack, oh Jesus, Jack, when he appeared that evening for dinner – Anthony likes a formal sit down when we have guests, produces his finest vintage wine – Carl was dressed in a formal suit and was completely bald. Then he looked right at me and . . . winked.'

The waitress, concerned, appeared, asked,

'Is everything all right?'

I gave her my best smile – it's a blend of thank you and fuck off – said,

'Absolutely, my friend here just got promoted to Sergeant in the Guards.'

Cops?

She took off.

This was a people who'd believed in Lech Walesa.

We got out of there and Ridge produced a pack of Silk Cut, lit one with a trembling hand, apologized with 'I know, I shouldn't be smoking.'

I took one, lit up, said,

'Nicotine is the least of our problems.'

As we walked towards the Spanish Arch, she linked my arm.

It felt good.

She asked,

'So who is he, Jack?'

I said,

'Wrong question. Not who . . . *what?*'

We reached the memorial there near the bridge to the lost seamen, and I said that some people just liked to see everything burn.

She asked if that was one of Stewart's Zen lines.

'No, it's Michael Caine in *The Dark Knight.*'

We watched the swans for a while and her face was like a little girl's, her delight in those creatures as basic as good nature.

She looked at her watch, nice slim gold Patek Philippe.

Anthony obviously still had some funds.

She said,

'I'm on duty soon.'

I nodded, feeling the old pang for the career I'd lost.

'What are we going to do, Jack?'

I stayed with the same movie, said,

'Kill the batman.'

20

'God's humour tends to the dark side of life.'

KB

I've also been holding off about Father Ralph.

Why?

Because I liked him.

When Malachy told me of his demise, I was utterly lost.

I'd never expected to meet a priest I not only liked but respected, and I'd truly thought I could relate this earlier.

I couldn't.

Does it seem out of synch?

That's how it felt and that's how it will always feel.

I can only tell it after time has put some distance there.

If I hadn't met him, I'm in no doubt he'd be still alive.

That's a given.

So perhaps you can understand why I'm telling this in flashback – or in truth, in cowardice.

Plus it gives a feel of how Xanax and booze and the Devil distort everything.

Works for Paul Auster, so who am I to argue?

*

The morning started with all that luring promise of an Irish fine day.

You know it won't last.

Dress lightly and yup, you'll be drenched in jig time.

But you buy into this crap.

Why?

Otherwise you'd believe it rains all the time.

It does.

I was having me morning coffee – none of that latte shite, a double espresso and no sugar.

Was it bitter?

Like me heart.

I was going through the bookcases, trying to find an answer to Carl, to Kurt, to the Devil. Settled on this from that bastion of depressed priests, St Augustine:

Everyone who knows that he is doubting, knows something that is true, and about the thing he knows, he is certain. Everyone therefore, who doubts whether there is truth, has something true in himself, which he may not doubt.

I sat back, mused on this, sipped at the coffee and wondered if a Xanax would clarify it.

Did the X anyway and brewed more caffeine.

The sun was still conning us, of that I could be certain, so I headed out after the X kicked in.

How long since I'd been in a church?

Let's say they still used the Latin version of the Mass, was when.

What drove me in?

No, not Augustine, I'm certain.

Rain and desperation.

I'd been feeding the swans.

As a Galwegian, there are certain things you do:

1. Talk shite.

2. Never answer a question.

3. Stay the fuck away from notions.

4. Feed the swans.

The heavens opened and down came teeming torrents.

And yeah, I'd bought into the con of the early sun.

Was wearing a light wind-breaker, T-shirt featuring Barack, my perennial 501s, Converse trainers and no hat.

No warning, of course, so you could dive for shelter.

Just lashed down like the last refrain of the song 'Expectation'.

The Claddagh church has always been one of me favourites. The Dominicans had done one wondrous job on the restoration.

The church was nigh on empty.

One bent-over old lady doing the Stations of the Cross.

She seemed transfixed on the seventh.

I lit candles for my dead.

That took a time, not to mention a fair whack of Euros.

I was drenched, rain leaking from my hair down into the collar of my T. As I knelt before the array of candles, I tried to summon up the right prayer.

I had nothing, save 'God mind ye well.'

Least I meant it.

I took a pew near the altar, and like the government, decided to sit out the deluge.

I never heard the priest approach.

They'd become the stealth bombers of our nation.

That or be crucified.

He gave me a start. Realizing, he said,

'God forgive me, I didn't mean to give you a fright.'

Way too easy to utter, *Ye've been doing it for centuries.*

I nodded.

Wetly.

He was tall, mid fifties, full head of white hair, thin, in need of spuds and bacon.

I said,

'I'm used to frights.'

He gave a lovely smile. Then asked if he might sit for a moment with me.

If he wanted money, he'd have to raid the candle gig.

I said,

'Your church.'

Sounded more bitter than I intended, but I was wet and cold and not in need of a homily. *The Waltons* were on DVD if I needed that shite.

The smile again – could get on your nerves a bit. He said,

'God's, actually.'

Wrong programme. I should have said *Little House on the Prairie.*

He indicated the barrage of candles.

'You must have a long list.'

I could have said, *And you have a long fucking nose.*

But it was a church.

To rattle him, or just the bad drop in me, I said,

'I'm trying to neutralize fifty black ones someone lit in my home.'

Worked.

He was rattled.

'Mother of God.'

I don't in fairness think he could lay it on her.

I didn't reply, so he asked,

'Why on God's blessed earth would somebody do such a . . .'

He couldn't find an adequate description so I supplied,

'Diabolical?'

Nice to help a priest and gets you all kinds of good shit in the hereafter. I even added,

'A fiend.'

He was nodding, like he could see it, said,

'Exactly. That's precisely the term.'

A priest tells you that you're so correct, watch yer wallet.

As I was on a clerical roll, so to speak, I said,

'Left a headless dog too.'

That did him in entirely.

Horrified, he made the sign of the cross.

'In *Ainm an Athair*,

An Mhic,

Agus,

An Sirioaid Naoimh.'

Said it aloud in Irish, In the Name of the Father . . .

I was impressed with his Irish. He spoke like a native speaker.

They were as rare as decency.

I could see he was wondering if perhaps joining me had been such a smart move.

There was just us two in the church now.

The old woman had packed it in on the eleventh Station, and who could blame her?

He ventured,

'Might I pry into what in God's heaven would possess a person to do such an act?'

Possess?

How apt.

I told him most of the story, omitting my . . . retaliation.

I know the clergy is big on retribution, but retaliation?

I painted a fairly comprehensive picture of Carl/Kurt and his minions.

He muttered,

'The Devil's minions.'

I almost slipped, *Good name for a rock band, yah think?*

Instead, I concluded with,

'There is a Ban Garda – actually a Sergeant now – and she can verify everything I've told you, lest you think I'm a raving lunatic.'

It wasn't that he didn't hear me, he clearly did, but in his face, something had changed. He was remembering something he had hidden and wished it had stayed thus.

My dripping clothes had formed a pool of water at our feet. He stood and said,

'You poor man, you're drenched and perished. Come on, I'll get you a towel in the Sacristy.'

The inner sanctum.

Dan Brown, eat yer heart out.

Could be, he intended calling the Guards.

I followed him along the altar, genuflected when he did before the Holy Sacrament and remembered a lovely line,

'Walk gently as you walk on Holy ground.'

He opened a heavy oak door, ushered me in.

Took a set of keys from his cassock, bent down, fiddled with a lock and then produced not only a fine thick towel but, get this,

a bottle of Bushmills –

and not just any old Bush,

Black Bushmills,

the holy grail of Irish whiskey –

two heavy glass tumblers, made of Galway crystal and, I shit thee not, with angels on the sides.

I dried me hair as he poured healthy measures into the glasses, handed me one, said, '*Is feidir liom.*'

Made me smile. What Barack said to our prime minister on St Paddy's Day.

'I am able.'

Would that we were.

My kind of priest. I said,

'*Bheannacht leat fein.*' (Blessing on yerself.) Added,

'No offence, but you're not the usual . . . how should I term it . . . clergy I'm used to.'

I put out my hand, said,

'Jack Taylor.'

He had a firm grip in more ways than one, said,

'Father Raphael – after the Archangel of Healing – but most people call me Ralph.'

Pity it wasn't Michael, who smote the demon, but you take what you get, like Bushmills.

Then a light went off in his eyes and he asked,

'Jack Taylor, who saved the swans?'

Saved is overstating it.

Through luck really, and a lot of sitting under Nemo's pier on miserable nights, I caught a psycho who was killing those beautiful creatures.

I, shall we say, smote him.

Last I heard, the said nutter was a doctor.

Go figure.

Ralph and I drank in what might have passed as comfortable silence.

Give me Black Bushmills, I'm comfortable.

He was taking my measure. Good luck with that. Long as he wasn't measuring out the Bushmills in the same way.

I could wait.

Then,

'I spent a lot of time in Africa, Jack, back in the days when priests were welcome. I saw a lot of things that don't have what you'd call a rational explanation.'

The recollection was hurting him, but he had a glass of the best, so he continued,

'I was down in the townships, in Jo'burg, and . . .'

He stopped. Poured us damn nigh lethal measures, then went on,

'There was a rash of killings there. Now bear in mind that killings and violence were, God forgive me, commonplace, but these were different. Young men and women were being killed, gutted and . . .'

He took a large sip, very large.

Me too.

'Headless dogs were sometimes found in the bellies of the deceased.'

Now it was like every breath of air had been sucked from the room.

And that to happen on Holy ground?

He took a deep breath, said,

'Jack, the natives – decent, lovely people – told me that the young people, the ones who . . . the ones who were butchered had been spending time with a man they referred to as Monsieur K.'

I had . . . nothing.

As Mr K might have put it,

'*Rien.*'

Save a warm glow from the fine booze. But I asked,

'What happened?'

He gave a resigned sigh, said,

'Monsieur K disappeared. The killings stopped and I prayed to God I'd never hear of him again.'

He was a priest – from what I could tell, an intelligent, level-headed, compassionate man. In my experience, such a person got fucked, one way or another.

You want to prosper?

Treat the world like the shite it is, then maybe, one day, if you meet a decent person, fuck him first.

But here was a man grounded in faith, taught Theology for what, seven years? And what do I know, maybe even Metaphysics. He knew stuff, had been freaking educated in it, so I asked,

'What do you think now, Father ... I mean, Ralph. This is way beyond coincidence, not to mention serendipity.'

He nodded, said,

'Tis sad, tis true, that's the Holy all of it.'

He was fucking kidding.

That air of resignation.

Where was the fight?

I mean, if the clergy hadn't an answer to evil, what the hell was a poor bastard like me meant to do?

Pray?

Do the Lotto?

I wanted to shake him, demand a solution. He was a priest, our moral guardian, and if he gave in, what hope did the rest of us poor schmucks have?

But he was so visibly shaken, I eased on me ferocity, took the bottle, gave him a blast.

He didn't even seem to notice.

The Sacristy had a beautiful stained-glass window and now a beam of light shone through.

You read a significance there?

Just Irish weather.

I said,

'The rain has stopped, I should go.'

I put the towel on the back of the chair, put out my hand, said,

'Thanks, Ralph, you've restored a lot of me faith in the Church.'

He walked me out, not saying a word. Outside, the sun having reappeared, the Claddagh Basin never looked so lovely.

For form's sake more than anything else, I asked,

'Any suggestions?'

I know defeat and despair, and it was mirrored here, and what had he got but cliché?

He took it.

I don't blame him.

He said,

'Ask God to rid us of this pestilence.'

I liked him, you've gathered that, but Jesus, I couldn't let it go. I couldn't. Asked,

'And if God lets more young people get killed?'

He reached in his cassock, pulled out his rosary beads like a coke head in need of the connection, muttered,

'Jack, we have to believe. Faith is what sustains us.'

Sounded just like the government.

I said,

'I have other options.'

21

'Always trust what your heart knows.'

Hafiz

Father Ralph was seriously disturbed by the encounter with Jack Taylor. And he felt that he had failed him. He went back into the church to say a decade of the rosary for the poor man.

He was startled to see a man in the front row.

A man with long golden tresses.

For a brief moment, he thought he'd imbibed too much of the Bushmills. It almost looked like Jesus!

Much as he'd always wished for divine intervention, he hadn't necessarily wanted it so directly.

Without turning, the man said in some kind of foreign-accented English,

'Rest easy, priest, I'm not the pale Nazarene.'

The urge to flee was paramount, but he drew on his will and the Bushmills. By God, he would not be intimidated in his own church.

The man had his feet up on the connecting pew, totally at his ease. He said,

'Take a load off, Ralphy, come join me.'

Ralph approached slowly and the man turned to look at him.

Yellow eyes.

It wasn't possible.

The man patted the seat, said,

'I'm not going to bite you . . . yet.'

Ralph stood in front of him, and had to admire the sheer quality of the suit.

The man said,

'Allow me to introduce myself.'

and laughed, said,

'Like the Stones song.'

Ralph felt a cold breeze rush down the aisle and nearly knock him over. He steadied himself, asked,

'Is there something I can help you with?'

The man ran his fingers through his hair, almost a sensuous gesture, said,

'You thought I couldn't enter a church.'

Then reached in his immaculate suit, took out a pack of cigarettes, lit one with a slim gold lighter, frowned and asked,

'Is it OK to smoke in the house of the dead Jew?'

Before Ralph could answer, the man blew a perfect ring towards him and said,

'I feel you were of little solace to our mutual friend.'

Ralph was more terrified than he'd ever been in his whole life. Not even the bad days of the township had affected him like this.

The man said,

'Ah, the township, now wasn't that a happening burg?'
Then asked,
'Cat got your tongue, priest?'
Ralph finally managed to say,
'I'm going to call the Guards.'
The man stood up, flicked his cigarette at Ralph's cassock, said,
'I think it's about five yards to the Sacristy, sure you want to risk it?'
He didn't.
Ralph, despite himself, sank down into the seat. The man smiled and said,
'Let me tell you a story. A parable, I think you guys call them?'
Ralph nodded, muttered,
'Parables, yes, that's right.'
The man reached over, touched Ralph on the face, the touch like the hand of the cemetery, said,
'See, we're bonding, already we've got us a dialogue going.'
He gave a smile, like the worst kind of madness, said,
'Thing is, priest, I have a special thing for our Mr Taylor. He has, mainly through bumbling, upset some playtime I had.'
Ralph wanted to move, to run, but he felt paralysed. The man said,
'And you, priest, filling his head with nonsense, with half-heard stories, now he is going to be even more of an irritant than I'd anticipated.'
He moved closer to Ralph, said,

'But all this seems very heavy, am I right?'

Ralph tried to smile and hoped maybe the lunatic was going to leave, but the man said,

'I get a very bad press, and really, I'm a fun guy. You like tricks, Ralphy?'

Ralph managed to utter a yes. He knew if you could keep a psycho on your side, you had a shot.

The man said,

'Wonderful, I do love a player. Watch this.'

And clicked his fingers.

A noose appeared above the statue of Saint Jude. Last resort of hopeless cases.

'Just for the hell of it, you're going to hop on up there, put that around your ecclesiastical neck and swing as if you meant it.'

Ralph felt his limbs move and he was walking towards St Jude. The man said,

'Swing for the sinner, daddy-o.'

Outside, the man stood for a moment, re-living how Taylor had fucked up his little diversion of the boy who'd been beheading swans.

An elderly woman approached, looked towards the church and asked,

'Would you know if Father Ralph is in residence?'

He gave her his most charming smile, said,

'He's a little tied up right now.'

She looked crestfallen and he asked, his accent deliberately more foreign,

'You are Catholic, no?'

She was indignant, said,

'Born and bred, and proud of it.'

Oozing charm, he asked,

'I'm a stranger to your country and, forgive me, to your religion.'

She was thinking, *Protestant, they can't even speak right*. But she was prepared to be Christian. She said,

''Tis not your fault.'

He had to force himself not to laugh, said,

'You might be able to help with me with a question about your faith.'

She was delighted. Jesus and His Holy Mother, she might make a convert. She said,

'Ask away.'

'They say – please forgive my English, but suicide is the one unforgivable sin in your belief?'

She nodded furiously, said,

'Oh that's the big one, no coming back from that one, damned for all eternity.'

He moved right up to her, and she thought his breath smelled funny, like wilted flowers. He said,

'Then if you will pardon my French, your Father Ralph is fucked.'

On St Patrick's Day, a young student named, yes, Sarah, was found murdered in Eyre Square.

Didn't stop the parade, but OK, did delay it a little.

The head of a dog was found resting – gently, they tell me – on her gutted stomach.

That's when I finally decided to kill Carl/Kurt.

I was in my apartment when I heard the news. Got the call from Stewart.

Brief.

But then what was there to say?

I could already hear the brass bands, inevitable police sirens, ceilidh music, all intermingled as the madness of St Paddy's Day got into full whoop. We never needed an excuse, but if it was legit to get pissed, it got my vote.

I began to clean the Sig.

A clean gun is like prayer – it might not do the job, but you're en route.

I had me one sharp knife, a throwback to my glory days of the swans, and it's sharp as a nun on her second sherry.

I carved crosses on to the head of the bullets.

Makes them like hollow points and it seemed appropriate.

I was all out of silver bullets and gee, guess what, they're a whore to find.

Mostly I needed a bloody miracle.

I lit another cig, and my mobile shrilled.

Answered.

'Jacques, *comment ça va?*'

I said, as I jammed the cartridge into the Sig,

'*La Feile Padraig.*'

'*Excusez moi?*'

'It's Irish for Happy St Patrick's Day.'

A pause, then,

'How lovely, and how fitting with my rather excellent news.'

I put the cig in the ashtray, asked,

'What news is that, good buddy?'

He gave that viper laugh, I could feel the iciness over the line, said,

'You are going to the US of A. *Félicitations, mon frère.*'

I could laugh or puke. Went,

'When?'

He caught the curtness, said,

'May the thirteenth. You are happy, *n'est-ce pas?*'

'Delirious, but I owe you, bro. Where are you staying? I'd like to show my real appreciation.'

Again the laugh, but with a somewhat dulled vigour.

'I've been with Anthony and his delightful wife, but as you know, guests are like fish, they stink after three days.'

The emphasis on *stink* was not lost.

I looked out at the nuns' convent, held the gun up against the faint light, asked,

'So, you are staying?'

He gave a theatrical sigh, said,

'I have the penthouse at the Meyrick. Are you familiar with it?'

I said,

'So sorry that poor girl was murdered almost on your doorstep.'

Formerly the Great Southern, the Meyrick overlooked Eyre Square.

His tone now in a different arena, he said,

'*Quel dommage.*'

I pushed, said,

'And a dog's head, damn gruesome, don't you think?'

Real granite coming down the phone now.

'I never cared for *les chiens*.'

I upped my bright tone, asked,

'So Carl, my benefactor, would tomorrow at seven be suitable for a farewell dinner? My treat, of course. I'll wait for you in the lobby.'

His blitz was back.

'*Bien sûr*. We'll have us a good time.'

I nearly added,

'I'll leave the dog at home.'

No need to tip my hand.

I hung up.

Those two damn cigs I'd smoked with Peg, the tinker lady, you got it, I was hooked again. Add to the mix:

Xanax,

Jay,

Guinness,

and now fucking nicotine.

Even had me a new Zippo.

How'd that happen?

I'd had a few over me limit and lit up, so to speak, I'd gone into Holland's. One of the few remaining old shops and still holding, despite the recession. Mary, a dote, had been there as long as I could remember. Not once, ever, did I see the slightest dent in her natural good humour.

Jesus, she had to have her share of troubles, but did she once take it out on the customers?

Nope.

A saint.

She'd be mortified if you told her.

I didn't.

I bought a brass Zippo with the Claddagh emblem. Mary offered to gift-wrap it. I said no, it would be fine.

She said,

'I fuelled it for you, Jack.'

If only they did Mary in a patch, you could erase depression overnight.

Now I was clicking it, loving that clunk that only a Zippo has. Rang Stewart, asked,

'How's Aine?'

He laughed, asked,

'You write her name down, Jack?'

Er . . . yes.

'C'mon Stewart, she's important to you, I know her name.'

A cynical laugh, then,

'What's up?'

Sounding like that old Bud advert.

I said,

'I'm meeting Carl, he's staying at the Meyrick, I'm buying him dinner.'

'The where?'

'Used to be the Great Southern, Gerry Barrett owns it. He also owns the Eye cinema and the Benetton outlet, and Edward Square is named after his dad.'

He said,

'I know Gerry, good guy.'

I asked as I used the Zip to fire up,

'Anyone you don't know?'

Pause, then,

'Times are, Jack, I don't think I know you at all. Hey, what was that sound? Are you smoking again?'

What was he going to do, tell Aine on me? I lied,

'You fucking kidding me? You know how hard I found it to quit.'

He let it slide, then,

'You're meeting with him again? Why?'

I was a bit pissed about the cig remark so I hit back with the truth.

'I'm going to kill him.'

Silence.

Then,

'Jack, this is a joke, right? Please tell me you're not serious.'

I told him about Peg, the priest, Father Raphael, South Africa and, lest he forget, his own responses to Mr K.

I flicked the Zippo back and forth. Stewart had been a dope dealer, he knew the sound of addiction.

I don't think I ever heard Stewart plead, not a trait you use when you've done hard time in Mountjoy and you were a pretty boy going in.

He pleaded now.

'Jack, listen to me, this is all conjecture. I'll admit there's some weird stuff going on, and sure, you can see a pattern of some very bad karma, but you've been doing a lot of dope, and I know it's been a very bad time with not getting into America and all, but . . .'

Pause.

'To cap a guy on speculation?'

Cap?

What were we? Boyz in the fuckin' hood?

I reined in a whole range of anger, assumed a patient tone, not easy for me, said,

'It has to end, Stewart.'

He took a deep breath, Zenning no doubt, and said,

'What if you're way off base? You're going to kill a man on . . . on what is probably a terrible set of coincidences, and I hate to say this, Jack, your own peculiar paranoia.'

Long silence as we both measured what we should say. I went with,

'I'm guessing you won't be available as back-up?'

Deep distress in his voice, he said,

'Aine is a very fine lawyer. You're going to need one.'

I asked,

'What makes you think I'll be caught?'

Total resignation as he said,

'Cos, Jack, you fuck up everything.'

Hung up.

He was the closest to a real male friend I had, so I figured I'd at least consider his point.

I remembered a time, after I'd been thrown out of the Guards, I was drinking like Behan in his last days and not giving a fuck. I met an American in a pub on Forster Street.

In publishing, if I remember, and we got to chatting about the nature of evil.

It was a pub, so what'd you expect?

He was editing a book on the supernatural and told me:

'It's known as horror. Occult fiction. I call it the Further-Out genre, like in David Lynch movies. You're in the middle of a crime story. But then the camera finds, say, a painting. Pushes into it. Turns a corner into the realm of the metaphysical. Which, in the sense of the real origins of suspense, might actually take us closer than men with guns ever could.

Consider.

Everyone sees things out of the corner of their eye. Everyone has feelings that can't be explained. Everyone, to a certain extent, is afraid of the dark. The Further-Out genre speaks to this condition. Reminds us that maybe, at essence, if a gun is pointed at you, it's not the bullet you're afraid of.

You're afraid for your soul.'

His name was John something or other. I remember his words so clearly, as I was stunned a young guy could know so much.

Over the years, I kept a vague track of his career and wasn't surprised he'd become an editor with some major American publisher.

I wish I'd kept in touch.

22

'What warehouse of the soul awaits me now?'

KB

How to dress for murder?

Neatly.

I put on me finest suit. That it is me only suit is a minor quibble.

Nice clean shirt (charity shop) and a Masonic tie I'd . . . er . . . acquired.

Cloud the issue.

Some gel in me hair. Slicked.

The Sig in me waistband.

Dropped two X, muttered,

'Time to kill.'

John Grisham needed the promo.

Bought a bottle of Moët.

See, you can teach an old dog new tricks, albeit expensive ones.

I entered the hotel, asked for Carl and was told,

'Penthouse, top floor, you are expected.'

The Masonic tie?

I wasn't sure if he'd meet me as the elevator opened.

Me experience of penthouses is a little limited.

He didn't.

Long as I live, and that's always up for grabs, I was surprised the penthouse had a number.

101.

Most hotels – forget the stuff about not having a thirteenth floor – never have a room with that number because of Orwell's *1984*. That room is where you find the thing you are most afraid of. There is even a TV show based on it, where celebrities get to dump their pet hates.

The door to the penthouse was open, so I went in.

I had no fixed plan as to how this was going to go down. Basically, shoot the bollix and run.

Company.

Not in me plan.

Two gorgeous girls.

Snorting coke, lines of it on a beautiful glass table.

Washing it down with bubbly.

Carl appeared, in a silk dressing gown that the Hef would have been proud of. Beaming, he said,

'Jack, meet the girls.'

Ingrida and . . . yes, Tricia.

Hookers.

East Europe's best.

I handed over the Moët, he slapped my shoulder, said,

'You kill me.'

The guy had style – repellent, but fuck it, he had the moves. He said,

'Room service is about to provide us with a veritable feast.'

Did I do the decent thing?

As in leave?

No.

I did the coke, had the amazing food, the more amazing hooker, and come two in the morning,

sated,

drunk,

doped,

the girls left.

Carl/Kurt, sprawled on the white leather sofa, his legs spread, eyes afire, said,

'*Une nuit excellente.*'

I took out the Sig, levelled it.

He smiled, said,

'Ah Jacques, you disappoint. Is this the gratitude you express to your *bon ami, votre frère?*'

I said,

'I was going to ask you to do the trick with the blond locks, but you know? Who the fuck cares.'

He gave that wild laugh, was mid sentence,

'Ah, the hair that is—'

I shot him in the balls.

First.

Then, moving over, I shot him in the guts, said,

'Sorry, all out of dogs' heads.'

I swear to Christ, he was smiling, so I ended that by opening his mouth, shot him right in those terrific teeth.

I checked his pulse, none.

Then moved to his bedroom, took

the Rolex,
the Mont Blanc,
a damn nigh mountain of coke,
a wadge of cash such as I'd never seen,
then got the fuck outa there.

Took the emergency stairs, met nobody, and once I was out on the street, I exhaled.

Jesus.

I've killed before.

I still have dreams about it, about them.

Back in my apartment, sure, I did some fine coke, tried on the Rolex.

Does that sound cold?

Hello, it's fucking unreal, is what it felt.

Murder and sex.

Pure noir.

The last time I got sex, the *Titanic* was a viable option.

Instead of being wired, I was out of it, like this happened in a bad B-movie.

I did some X to chill.

Put on the TV, Living channel, and no, the title wasn't wasted on me.

They were showing series two of *Supernatural*.

The two brothers, they killed the demon in the three episodes I watched.

Maybe in series three, they'd get it right.

I hoped to fuck I got it right in the only series I'd get.

*

I waited the next morning to be arrested.

Even dressed for it.

No watch.

Just jeans and a T-shirt.

When the Guards came crashing through my door, macho shite at the fore, I'd be ready.

The Sig, unloaded, sitting on the table.

Me on the other side of the room, so they wouldn't have to shoot me.

I wouldn't even plead, just go, take the shite. Whatever sentence they imposed, I'd been serving it for years anyway.

I could at least read in relative peace.

Bottom line, as love was out of the question, it was all I ever really wanted.

They didn't come.

And I waited.

They didn't come.

Drank some strong black coffee, smoked more cigs than I intended, but then you always do, and finally grabbed the phone, rang the Meyrick.

An Irish receptionist.

The recession was truly biting.

A year ago, an Irish person working in a hotel? Nope.

I asked for Carl and was told,

'He checked out.'

I wanted to scream,

'I know, I fucking checked him out permanently.'

Kept it together, asked,

'You checked him out personally?'

Keeping it light.

She said patiently,

'No, automatic checkout, the bill is put under the door and all the client needs to do is drop off the key.'

I clicked off.

What the fuck was going on?

Did his minions sneak him away?

I did a few lines of his coke, the Rolex sliding nicely along my wrist.

The coke was primo.

Christ, that ice drizzle down the back of your throat, the world literally crystallizes and you can do what-the-fuck-ever you ever dreamed.

Like the God-awful song, 'I Can See Clearly Now'.

I rang Stewart, didn't bother with the 'How yah doing' shite, launched,

'Carl checked out this morning.'

His relief was evident. He said,

'Jack, I'm so glad you saw sense, didn't do ... you know.'

Holy fuck.

I said,

'Listen up, you Zen-besotted eejit, he checked out this morning but I checked *him* out at two a.m.'

Long silence, then,

'Jack, you need help, you have seriously lost the plot. I know some people ...'

I cut in,

'I shot him three times, and right now I'm sampling his coke, wearing his Rolex . . .'

He hung up.

I paced.

A lot.

Coke zig, fear, exhilaration, disbelief, Xanax, touch of the Jay.

Didn't help.

I switched on the TV. Moved quickly past the Jerry Springer show, stopped for a brief moment at the sitcom *Rules of Engagement* as the guys outlined the specifics for a real guy weekend.

The one I liked, or the coke loved, was 'Never, *never* admit to having seen *Brokeback Mountain.*'

If ever a sentence nailed the Irish male psyche, there it was.

Moved on to the news.

Liam Neeson's wife had been tragically killed.

I couldn't handle that.

Moved on.

More awful tidings.

'The Real IRA claimed responsibility for murdering two young British soldiers.'

And I thought I'd killed the Devil.

Two young engineers were heading for Iraq.

I dreaded the retaliation this would bring.

And local news: more jobs being lost, redundancies daily.

I muttered,

'The eighties are back.'

Duran Duran were highly successful all over again.

Oh fuck.

U2 were pissed as they'd hit Number One in every country save Finland.

Those Finns, eh?

I sat at the kitchen table, the Zippo clicking in my hand, the Sig, I swear still warm to the touch, close by.

There was a tree right outside the window, almost overlooking the nuns' convent, and I watched a tiny bird flit from branch to branch.

Saint Martin's little bird, they called him.

I was, I know, deferring.

Great word, means you're trying like the be-jaysus not to dwell on the topic that is dominating your every thought.

I got out an A4 pad, tried to list all the stuff that had gone down since my first meeting with Kurt/Carl.

Took me close to an hour.

I timed it on the flash Rolex.

That was real.

Right?

Had me some pit stops, as opposed to pitfalls.

One double espresso,

a Xanax,

three cigs,

and what had I got?

Not a whole lot.

Was he the Devil?

Did I kill the Devil?

I know, it's as crazy as it sounds and looks.

So . . . what to do?
The sun came blasting through the window.
Lit up the whole apartment, and right then I knew.
Let
it
go.

23

Post-Armageddon

Here is what you might term the aftermath.

Stewart got engaged to his lawyer.

Bought her a rock the size of Gibraltar.

The killings stopped.

Ridge stayed married and the business deal evaporated.

Guess they'll have to sell another horse.

Anthony is Anglo-Irish, they don't do poverty, not in my sense.

And me, on a whim I just went to London, on an internet all-inclusive package. I sold the Rolex in Camden Lock, the guy screwed me and I said,

'Devil of a price.'

I met a woman.

An American, in her forties, she liked the sound of me voice and she liked to drink Jay.

She liked nothing better than to breeze about books, movies and music.

She is coming over to stay with me at Easter.

We had us a real fine time.

Prowled the second-hand bookstores and music shops.

I bought

Sexy Beast,

Home for the Holidays (directed by Jodie Foster),

Mad Men, series one.

In the bookstores, I found a rare Aleister Crowley tome. First edition, too.

I'd had enough of the beast.

Sunday, at Heathrow, I was glowing from the night before with my new lady. Thinking,

'How the fuck did that happen?'

But grateful.

Waiting for my flight to be called, I found a tabloid on the table as I finished my black coffee. Flicking through to see if Chelsea had won, I spotted – almost missed – on page six:

A student at LSE has been found murdered. The details of his death have been withheld. The Metropolitan Police are anxious to interview a Mr K, who was the last person seen with the deceased.

My flight was called.

I put the paper aside, wondered how the UK would deal with the Devil.

Probably figure he was Irish.

A week later, I'd just settled into my sleep when the phone rang.

It was the lady in my life and I was delighted to hear her.

Outlined the things we'd be doing in Galway till she said,

'Jack, strange thing, can I share?'

God bless America, they sure do know how to share. I said,

'Hon, course you can.'

She said,

'This is going to sound like I'm a whack job, but I woke late last night and there was a black candle burning on my bedside table. What should I do?'

I took a deep breath, checked where the Sig was, said,

'Sweetheart, blow it out.'